Hearts Without Homeland: Roots In Exile

JEAN FRANCOIS CHEUWA

ISBN: 978-1-972004-23-4

Acknowledgements

I am very grateful to everyone who made this book project possible.

My deepest regards to some persons (elders) in Cameroon who enlightened my knowledge about some cultural facts discussed in the book. I am also grateful to my friend Carla from Guatemala, who taught me a lot about her country's culture, traditions, and wisdom through tales from her country. My large family in Cameroon and abroad, including my Mum, siblings, and friends, was a big inspiration for me when I initiated this project. Please accept my heartfelt thank you.

Lastly, I would like to dedicate this work to all those who endure the hardship of exile. May the story narrated in this book enlighten each and everyone.

Dedication

To my lovely wife, Francine, for understanding and being patient with me during this project.

To my children, Michel, Ashley, and Zoe, your love of reading and books inspires me and pushes me to keep going until the end of this project.

About the Author

Jean Francois Cheuwa was born in Bandja, in Cameroon's western region. After his Baccalauréat in 2001, he was accepted at the University of Dschang, where he earned a BA in History of International Relations in 2005. After, he pursued a Maîtrise of History of International Relations at the University of Yaoundé and later obtained a DEA in Political and Cultural History from the University of Ngaoundéré in 2009. In 2021, he obtained a master's degree in French and Francophone literature and Cultures from Florida State University.

Jean-François's love of writing began in his early years, when he wrote a variety of poems and stories. His prior reading and personal life experiences lead him to fall in love with the concepts of exile, roots, resilience, displacement, identity, and belonging. His journey at Florida State furthered and reinforced his desire to write about them. He is currently in the last year of a PhD in Educational Leadership at Florida Agricultural and Mechanical University in Tallahassee, Florida.

Prologue

The forest did not ask where he came from. It did not care for passports or papers, nor did it flinch at the weight of his exile. It only whispered softly, endlessly through the leaves, as if to say: You are not lost. You are becoming. He walked beside her, the woman with eyes like river stones and a voice that carried the scent of home, though he had never known her country. They did not speak much. Words were heavy then. But silence, shared in the hush of the trees, was sacred. Each step away from the camp was a step toward something unnamed. Not freedom, not yet, but possibility. And when the forest opened its arms to them, when the birds sang in languages older than borders, and the wind braided their stories together, they knew: They were no longer fugitives. They were seeds. And somewhere, in the soil of exile, they would grow.

Contents

Acknowledgements v
Dedication vi
About the Author vii
Prologue viii
Chapter 1: The Path of Legacy and Hope 1
Chapter 2: Crossing Horizons 5
Chapter 3: Growing Roots 9
Chapter 4: The Day the Mask Fell 12
Chapter 5: The Border That Broke Him 15
Chapter 6: The Girl with River-Stone Eyes 18
Chapter 7: Whispers in the Camp 23
Chapter 8: The Forest of Becoming 27
Chapter 9: The Samaritan 33
Chapter 10: The Village of Forgotten Names 38
Chapter 11: Seeds of Trust 43
Chapter 12: Nostalgia and Nightmares 48
Chapter 13: The Circle of Hands 53
Chapter 14: Quetzals and Lions 58
Chapter 15: The Crown of the Exile 63
Chapter 16: Embracing the Inner Land 68
Chapter 17: Two Kingdoms, One Heart 73
Chapter 18: The Wedding Under the Ceiba Tree 78
Chapter 19: Roots and Reveries 83
Chapter 20: Echoes of the Ancestors 87

Chapter 21: Roots in Exile 91
Poem 1: Roots of Resilience 95
Poem 2: Heritage's Flame 97
Poem 3: The Tapestry of Unity 99
Poem 4: Land and Spirit 101
Poem 5: Love Beyond Borders 103
Author's Note 105
Letter to readers 106

Chapter 1: The Path of Legacy and Hope

Njegwe was born in the green hills of western Cameroon, where the earth itself seemed saturated with his ancestors' spirits. He was born into the royal lineage of his village, and as a baby, he was rocked to sleep with tales of kings and warriors, of sacred forests and of ancestor spirits who protected their people. And since childhood, he learned that his blood bore the burden of a legacy, and a sacred obligation to honor the land, the spirits, and those who'd come before him for generation upon generation.

His father was a wise and humble king who both led and protected tradition. The royal compound was not just a home and a haven; it was a living testament to history, drums, elders' stories about kings whose spirits roamed the sacred groves, incense, and burning wood in the air. Every spot in their compound was holy, every ceremony a stitch in the fabric of who they were.

Growing up, Njegwe was taught that leadership was about service, humility, and respect for the land. The days were taken up with formal schooling at the village school, where he was among the best pupils, and informal training under the shade of sacred trees. His grandmother, the family matriarch, would sometimes sit beneath the broad branches of the Kola tree and, in calm but stern tones, tell stories that blurred the line between myth and history. She would say the land was alive, that its roots held the memories of their people, and that to respect the land was to honor the spirits that inhabited it.

His years at the University of Yaoundé were pivotal, a time of awakening outside his village. There, among students from Cameroon's entire country, Njegwe's horizons broadened. He worked hard, aiming to improve people's conditions and bring traditional progress. His graduation was a bright spot, a recognition after years of sacrifice and hope. He waved his diploma in the air, understanding it wasn't just a piece of paper, but a holy thing, an emblem of his ancestors' and his neighborhood's dreams.

With a degree in hand, Njegwe began working at a local bank. The new building, humming with the artificial sound of modernity – clacking keyboards, ringing phones, and hurried footsteps was a far cry from the hallowed forests of his youth. However, in this new world, he bore the vigor of the old one. His relationship with his father was a beacon, a source of wisdom from kings and the sacred duties they enforced.

For five years, Njegwe toiled away, rose through the ranks, saved every franc, and dreamt softly of a time when he would be able to serve not just his community but also seek new ways to elevate his people. Yet underneath the calm existence that passed for life, a secret unrest haunted him, suggesting foreign lands; whispering of beyond-the-seas country and beyond-the-river wonders which lay betwixt him and the world he often wished to see.

Those whispers grew louder over time, fables from friends, news from the diaspora, and stories of a land called America. The stories created a vision of possibility: cities alive with diversity, innovation, and hope. It was a place where dreams were born, and grew, and for that steady boy from the tiny village to become somebody bigger. But he also knew that visions like that were made of more than longing; they were made of courage, determination, and conviction.

And so Njegwe started thinking daringly: applying for a visa to the United States. The idea was not only exhilarating but also terrifying, an act of faith which could alter his life forever. The process was grueling; every form, every interview, was a gut check of his determination. It was a maze to navigate, with immigration laws dictating the path; each rejection or delay was the system's doing, another hurdle to overcome. At night, he would say silent prayers under the star-filled sky, beseeching the spirits of his ancestors for protection and guidance.

He remembered the tales his father recounted about kings who suffered exile and hardship but never lost their dignity. He drew strength from such stories, recognizing that real leadership was defined by resilience. With each barrier, he learned to turn hope into determination, to see defeat not as a stumbling block but as a stepping stone.

Months of waiting, of hope and fear teetering on a knife's edge, finally arrived in the form of a flimsy envelope, an approval, and with it, a pledge that his journey was feasible. The visa was tender parchment, but to Njegwe it was smack: a sacred scroll, a symbol of faith and an emblem of his hope that his dreams were not out of reach.

With great care, he packed his small possessions, selecting each one lovingly and blessing the memory. His heart overflowed with gratitude and eager expectation, for he felt that this parting was a holy one. The land of his birth dwindled below the clouds as the plane readied to lift off, leaving behind sacred forests, a royal compound, and tales of kings and warriors.

Njegwe looked out the window at the sky as the plane taxied down the runway and said to himself, "The earth of Cameroon, that so familiar and sacred earth, passed into a dim recollection." Yet inside him, the tales of his ancestors still echoed, and dim whispers of holy groves that had been, and the power of kings smoldered alive. It was more than a transoceanic voyage; it was a holy leap of faith, a pilgrimage that transcended hope, resilience, and the indomitable spirit of his legacy.

Chapter 2: Crossing Horizons

Njegwe's departure from Cameroon was another act of faith. Underneath this sacred kola tree that had seen many generations, he muttered prayers in Fe'efe'e, which was the same language that his ancestors spoke. He was sad and hopeful, for he felt that the crossing of the physical and spiritual was a holy bridge. He felt he was guided by the spirits of his land and ancestors; their whispers played in his head as he set out for what lay ahead.

The flight across the Atlantic was a passage through cloudiness and infinite water moving silently into nothing. Njegwe peered out the window and looked at the sea of scintillating blue that lay many feet below him: a vast expanse of possibility, peril, and promise. His mind wandered to his own childhood, to the sacred forests and rivers that whispered tales of kings and warriors. He felt the gravity of history and hope knotted in his chest, every mile widening the distance from the land of his birth but shortening the path to a new horizon.

The shift was immediate after the plane's landing at Washington Dulles International Airport. The air was new and fresh, with a strange yet appealing smell. The cityscape was a series of serrated checks against the morning sky, an edifice of steel and glass and far-off dreams. When he walked outside, the local traffic got enough bass from its engine to fill three city blocks and still hummed along in fine shape, with fuzzy sirens and an indistinct swirl of people's voices from every country on earth blending into a pleasing cacophony. Njegwe stepped onto the tarmac, his journey weighing on his bones, along with the whispers of his ancestors and the dreams of his people. His companion, who came to fetch him, took the wide avenues and concrete towers until he reached home. Where they got home, he was received with joyous songs, as his companions along with meals and beverages from the motherland.

His friend invited other Afro-communities members to the reception which extends into the early hours.

His first few days in Maryland were a whirlwind of discovery and adjustment. The streets vibrated with life, people scurrying past in clouds of color and tongue. Amidst the confusion, Njegwe found refuge in the silent corners of his mind, where he kept the stories of his country and ancestors alive. He drifted in and out of various communities where the drums and dance reverberated with the pulse beat of home. The bustling markets were filled with the scents of spices, smoky paprika, sweet cinnamon, spicy peppers, the aroma of roasted plantains and fresh mangos that took him back to Cameroon.

In these colorful environs, Njegwe formed a community with other Africans and Cameroonians who had crossed the seas in search of new lives. They regaled one another with steaming bowls of couscous manioc, couscous maïs, riz sauté, taro sauce jaune, and more. And their voices rose and fell in a language that made them feel they belonged. Elders told stories of resilience: how they had abandoned everything, carrying only hope and recollection, and built new roots in a foreign land. Their laughter was a balm to his still-tender spirit; their tears made it clear that exile was a burden, but also an unwritten bond.

As Njegwe tried to get a foothold in his new world, the task of finding a job became harrowing. The first few weeks were full of frustration, applications sent out on a prayer, interviews that revealed the chinks in his language skills, and moments when rejection seemed to murmur that maybe he didn't belong. Once, at a job interview, someone told him he would really struggle to get a job because of his accent, but Samuelson never gave up. Every morning, he woke up with determination, taking succor from the tales of kings who endured exile and never bowed, who, despite the bitterness of their fate, refused to stoop and posted guards in their hearts, in hope of a better day.

He came very close to returning home on a couple of occasions, but friends, especially his father, urged him not to go. At last, he got a low-paying gig as a cashier at the Nigerian-owned corner store. A few friends and countrymen helped him wade through the paperwork and social services web, some months later. It was a small victory, a sign that his determination came from a place deeper than ambition. It was a sacred imperative, handed down through his lineage, to make room and reason in this foreign place. Four months later, he secured a two-bedroom rented apartment of his friend, which fell within his pay range.

At night, Njegwe would sit silently in the small apartment and listen to the din of city cars, ambulances, and screams, as well as phones ringing with voices speaking various languages. He thought of the land he had abandoned, its sacred groves and rivers, its kings and servants, whose ghosts still murmured in the rustling leaves. Even though he had never heard the stories, they were there inside him, a flame hoarded and kindled as it would not burn.

In the course of time, he found others from his country, fellow Cameroonians, Nigerians, and Ghanaians, to form a small but resilient community. They shared cultural legends and traditional dances, and a common ambition to live lives grounded in their past. Njegwe found solace in that kinship, understanding that roots could never be limited to borders but might stretch deep into shared challenges and unbreakable traditions.

And in those times, Njegwe felt the silent presence of his ancestors guiding him. Their whispers also reminded him that resilience was an inheritance, something that could be reclaimed, even in exile. Maryland, and especially Silver Spring, where he found the apartment, was a land of opportunity, yes, but also a land of challenge. And in the silent power of his ragtag community, he was beginning to sow seeds for a new legacy, one rooted in hope, perseverance, and the unquenchable spirit of his ancestry.

Chapter 3: Growing Roots

For days, Njegwe's heart and hopes were lifted. Throughout his difficult journey, he saw each day as a chance to plant the seeds of hope in a future riddled with unpredictable outcomes. With every small win, from getting a job to making new friends, to finding happiness in the moments in between his resilience grew stronger, like a tree reaching for the sun.

He often liked to sit alone on the balcony of his humble apartment, calmly staring out at the city's lights. Traffic hummed in the distance, lights blinked or flickered against glass tabletops, and leaves rustled in soft gusts of air. During those silent periods, Njegwe meditated on his journey the lows, highs, and the lessons from every moment. The road had been fraught, but he knew that each step forward stood as a testament to the resilience of his character and the spirit of his ancestors.

One night, he arranged to meet his friends, Etienne from Cameroon and Deji from Nigeria, at a bustling African café near his apartment. There was the smell of roasted plantains, spicy peppers, laughter, and stories shared in equal measure. They sat outside under string lights, trading stories of home and still-to-be-realized dreams.

Etienne said to Njegwe, smiling widely, "You are successful already. You took less time than any of us here to succeed. Now, is it time to start thinking about inviting your father to visit?"

Deji smiled and nodded. "Yeah, brother. You have earned it. You are so strong and resilient, and I think that's inspirational. Your father would be very, very happy to see how well you are doing. You've built something here, and I think he would like to see it for himself."

Njegwe's eyes glistened with joy and hope. "I have been thinking about that an awful lot," he said quietly. "I want to invite him. Show him what I'm creating here, that his ancestors' strength is present in me. I want him to know that his son is strong, despite what we have been through."

The next day, Njegwe reached for his phone and called Cameroon. His father picked up after several rings, his tone steady and proud, full of warmth.

"Papa, how are my mother, siblings, and everybody?" Njegwe asked.

Before his father could answer, he continued, "I have been doing well." — Njegwe started, his voice shaking with emotion. "With my job at Walmart, I am saving every single penny so I can have you come visit me. I want you to see what the life I am trying to build looks like. I am planning to bring you here."

There was a soft silence on the line, and then his father's voice came through, warm with gratitude. "My son, I am very well. I am glad to see what you are becoming."

When he heard the words, Njegwe's heart soared. "Thank you, Papa. I can't wait to see you."

In the days that followed, hope sprouted afresh for Njegwe. He woke up every day with his head held high. His world was his work at Walmart, and when he arrived there, he would greet customers with a smile and a cheerful "Hey y'all!" To him, that small moment was proof of his own strength a minor triumph that encouraged him to persevere and believe in the possibility of a better future.

He spent a lot of time thinking about the community, the multiracial faces, the shared stories, the collective strength of people who, like him, had crossed oceans for a lottery ticket to something more. The joy of his life was lending a hand to others, sitting down to eat with them, and celebrating the cultural festivals that brought a bit of home into his new existence.

On the balcony in the evenings, Njegwe would watch the city lights twinkle and think about his ancestors. Their whispers resounded in his head, telling him that determination was an heirloom a thing which might be nourished anew, even in exile. Maryland, and Silver Spring in particular, where he had taken refuge, was a land of opportunity, yes, but also a land of challenges. Yet, out of perseverance and optimism, he felt he could create a new legacy.

He began frequenting community meetings, speaking about Cameroon and listening to other people's stories. These connections provided him with strength and a renewed sense of purpose. He learned that his strength was a gift he could give not just to himself, but to others. Each smile, each kind word, and every little victory became another root on which to stand.

And so, hopeful in his heart and guided by the whispers of his ancestors, Njegwe kept planting the seeds for his future, A future forged on hope, determination, and the indomitable spirit of those who came before him,. He understood that the journey was far from over, but he felt prepared to meet whatever came next with courage, faith, and the knowledge that, regardless of what else occurs, he is in the process of constructing something everlasting.

Chapter 4: The Day the Mask Fell

Njegwe's day started like any other, before dawn, with the dull hum of noise and the slow beat of routine, regular work. He walked out of his humble apartment on the way to Walmart, a mundane act infused with the longing for something better. The sun was just coming up, gold light spilling through the city streets.

But that morning was different.

A black van suddenly screeched to a halt beside him. Men in masks and black uniforms poured out to surround him. Hands seized him, and before he could realize what was going on, he was pushed into the car.

"ICE! Hands up!" a muffled voice commanded.

Njegwe's mind raced, confusion, fear, and disbelief coursing through him. He attempted to speak, to explain, but the officers worked with practiced efficiency. He was handcuffed and whisked away from everything he had worked so hard to build.

Fluorescent lights blinked overhead in the sterile detention center. The room could have been an alien, impersonal spaceship. They referred to him as "Case 47-B." Not a man, but a number. No trial, no reason given, no opportunity to say goodbye.

The days merged, the silence broken only by the distant tramping of guards' feet and by little whispered conversations among officials. His very name had been stricken from the record; his narrative was now just a file in a machine that could not recall humanity.

Then came the order, no warning, no explanation. He was flown to the south in a deportation camp, treated like discarded luggage. The roaring of the plane's engines filled his ears as he was lifted away from the community he had fought so hard to be a part of, the place he had come to call his second home.

He landed in El Salvadora foreign country that welcomed him with grim silence. The camp stank of rust and sweat. The walls were higher still, and in them the sound of emptiness, silence. Nobody spoke to him in his language. No one knew what would come next. He continued to grieve the mistake of leaving his native home, Cameroon, and for a long while, he began to miss his childhood, when he could smell and feel the scent of coffee plant residue in the breeze, blowing, rushing to the river indifferently with his sisters, and feel the simplicity of home. He also thought often of the royalty he had been born into, the life he had left behind to go to America, only to end up in this cage, in a foreign country, very far from everything he knew.

He took a seat on a cracked bench, blank eyes absorbing the weight of injustice, wrongful deportation, and a life interrupted. His dreams of the future in America had shattered in an instant. They had broken him down, but somewhere inside, a spark of resistance remained.

And then, in the midst of that bleakness, he saw her.

She was sitting by herself, doodling in the dust with a stick. She had tiny beads in her braids, and when he looked into her, he saw a challenge, the kind that might have passed silently between moon men in some lonely council hall.

"You're not from here," she whispered, speaking Spanish.

He hesitated, then nodded. "Cameroon."

She smiled. "Guatemala."

During that wordless exchange, something unsaid was exchanged between them, an understanding without words. A root that had reached under their common suffering.

That night, Njegwe dreamed of a forest whispering with wings and lost stories. She moved there in front of him, her footsteps faintly phosphorescent on the ground.

When he woke up, a new determination set in.

This was not the end.

It was the beginning.

Chapter 5: The Border That Broke Him

Njegwe's body was heavy with injustice the weight of his shattered dreams. The wrongful deportation had wounded him deeply, but beneath the pain, a small ember of determination refused to die. He had traveled across oceans and deserts, and hoped for America, every step fueled by the promise of a better life for himself and his loved ones back home.

He recalled the nights of hope, the days of labor, and the dreams he had entertained of a new life. But now, in this strange camp, that future felt distant, receding with each passing day. The guards' instructions were clipped and cold, bouncing off high, rusted walls that formed a chamber of despondency.

They referred to him as "Case 47-B." Just a tag on a file, stripped of even an ounce of humanity. Then, at dawn, he was shackled and loaded onto a plane, an unwilling party in a system that judged without allowing him to speak for himself. The sky smeared as the plane descended toward El Salvador, away from the land he had fought so hard to make his own.

When the time came for the plane to land, he was unceremoniously dumped at a bleak, desolate camp. The air reeked of rust and broken hopes. The guards' commands were clipped, their eyes blank. The silence that surrounded him seemed to storm and roar, a terror of stillness; in it, the voices of shattered lives, unremembered tales, clamored.

Njegwe crouched on the cold soil, staring downwards. Memories of Cameroon's forests, family, and sacred groves he had climbed as a boy surged through his mind. He remembered the sun on his face, the smell of coffee trees, and his siblings' laughter as they played to their heart's content. Still, one stubborn part of him refused to give in to despair.

He saw the others, faces lined with pain, hopes dying in mute anguish amid the dust. But in the midst of madness, he held on to one faint shard of something unbreakable: the belief that this could not be the end, and that somehow, beyond this hellhole, there was still a life.

And then, amid that silence, he saw her again.

She sat on a broken bench, sketching in the dirt with a twig. Her hair was in tiny, beaded braids, and her dark, wide, unafraid eyes stared back at him with a challenging calm.

"You are not from here," she said one more time, gently in Spanish.

He hesitated, then murmured. "Cameroon."

She smiled gently and said as she had stated before. "Guatemala."

No words needed to pass between them. In that moment, a silent understanding occurred, a realization of shared pain and strength. There was a root that ran beneath the chaos, binding two souls where others were desperate to forget.

The night descended slowly, and Njegwe found himself gazing up at the stars through the barbed-wire fences of the camp. Memories, Remembrances of home, of nights under the same sky, stirred within him desire and empathy for him. The stars told tales of ancestors and warriors who could not be bested.

That night, Njegwe dreamed once again of the forest whispering, teeming with wings and tales long unheard. She was leading, her footprints twinkling softly in the soil beneath her, shining a path for him to follow toward a place beyond pain and hopelessness.

When he woke up, she sat by his side with a steady gaze that seemed to say,

You don't know something yet.

"We're not supposed to be here," she said quietly.

"Nope," he responded, his voice hoarse with the emotion of the moment.

"Then let's go," she murmured, a quiet dare in her voice.

He looked at her, this girl with eyes of river-worn stone and saw not merely defiance, but something else: a spark of destiny burning inside her. They didn't have a plan, only an unspoken purpose, an unbearable hope whose presence flickered like a feeble flame in the darkness.

Sometimes, that's enough.

And that's when something dawned on Njegwe:

Deserted as he may be, no exiled man ever forgets the hearth; and from his own, he saw that the forests those old storytellers of red-mouthed Time awaited only life to cover themselves again.

Chapter 6: The Girl with River-Stone Eyes

Njegwe sat alone in the camp's flimsy shelter that night. Faint embers burning in a small fire, a little fire there, casting moving reflections on the walls. Outside, the distant hum of voices and the shuffle of footsteps composed an indistinct symphony, but inside, his mind was far away, deep into forests that no longer existed, into the home dear to recollection.

He closed his eyes and took a deep breath, and then he was there again. The air smelled of damp earth and fresh rain on well-dried soil. He heard the rustle of leaves, the low murmur of wind through tall trees, and the distant calls of birds in the canopy. He recalled the roughness of tree bark under his hands, sensing the life that pulsed through the ancient sacred groves of Cameroon.

In those forests, the trees were sentient, but more than just that: they were harbingers, preservers of memory.

He recalled climbing the iroko, kola, and ceiba trees with roots that reached deep into the earth, holding up generations of ancestors. The trees were fat and sturdy, their bark etched with stories of the elders who had gone before him. He could almost hear their words, low and rhythmic, whispering secrets only the brave would dare to guess.

He remembered the sensation of sunlight trickling through leaves, dappling him in patches of gold, and the cool shade that provided respite from midday scorch. There was life in the sacred groves, and the spirits within were silent; and he heard their stories by feeling their heartbeat beneath his fingertips. He knew they were watching over him. He was from the sacred forest, where trees and all the other elements of the wild carried a spirit.

Even there, in that remote camp, those roots would not break.

In the silence, he remembered everything: the strength of earth beneath him, the heartbeats pounding from below, the sacred hush of the woods, the stories written on every leaf and twig. Those memories were his ballast, his shield, the unbreakable connection to his homeland.

But the color faded as he became aware of his harsh new reality: the corroded fences, the strangers' faces, and the smell of sweat and iron that filled the camp. Yet inside him, deep down, a flame of resiliency burned on, stoked by the presence and fortitude of his childhood.

He opened his eyes. It was cold that night, but a tiny fire inside him burned stronger. Deep in the soil of those forests, in the hidden roots of his spirit, it still flourished.

A slight flutter in his periphery caught his attention. On the other side of the camp, a girl sat on a broken bench, drawing pictures in the dirt using trembling fingers. Her braided hair was threaded with tiny beads, and her dark eyes were calm and unafraid as they met his quietly.

She was drawing a tree above the ground, its roots in the soil, veins pulsing with life. Njegwe stared at her for a long moment and felt a connection.

"You dream of forests," he murmured, almost to himself.

She lifted her gaze, guarded but calm. "How do you know?"

Njegwe paused, then motioned to her sketchpad. "I can see it in your eyes; you seem like a person who fled from trees."

A half-smile played across her lips. "In my village, trees are stories, and they grow. The ceiba, my grandmother used to say, joins the heavens, earth, and underworld. I try to remember when I think, and when I draw. It is how I stay in touch through their stories."

He gazed into her eyes and carried his own memory. "I was born in a kingdom covered in forests, great, green, whispering with the voices of the dead. In western Cameroon, we feel the spirits of our forebears in those trees. I grew up climbing sacred groves, learning their stories, and feeling the earth's beat beneath me."

He paused, a trace of yearning in his expression. "When I stepped away, I held that forest within me, its roots and whispers. That's why I think the trees can talk if you listen hard enough. They are alive, not simply wood and leaves; they are the keepers of memory and history."

Catalina nodded, looking pensive and far away. "In Guatemala," she said quietly, "we think of the ceiba as a link between heaven, earth, and hell. As a child, I used to sit under its boughs and dream of the sky and the roots below my feet. "Occasionally, I felt, if I could just listen hard enough, my ancestors were in the leaves, whispering."

The silence became a comfortable presence; an unspoken accord wove between them, like roots extending deep into the soil that interlaced their tales. The night wore on with quiet reverberations of shared pasts and lingering ideals.

Then, at some point, Catalina reached into her pocket and revealed a small, fading scar on her wrist, a thin, crescent-shaped line.

"White folks tried to send me back," she murmured, her voice trembling. "Three times I ran. And each time, I came back stronger. They can imprison my body, but not my spirit."

He gazed into her eyes, knowing that the hungry gleam he saw there would not be extinguished. She was not merely a woman ensnared by a system; she was a survivor, a combatant who wore her defiance like a decoration.

That night, Njegwe dreamed again. It was a darker, denser forest, alive with whispers in tongues unknown to him. Catalina guided him through the darkness, her braid glowing dully, a lantern in the gloom. The trees appeared to breathe, their voices rising in a chorus that urged him to listen more intently. Their roots sank into the ground, holding secrets whispered across ten thousand years.

When he awoke, she sat next to him, with steady and unyielding eyes, as though she knew something he did not.

"We aren't supposed to be here," she said softly.

"No," he said, his voice husky with feeling.

"Then let's go," she murmured, a soft dare in her tone.

He gazed at her, this girl with river-stone eyes, and saw more than rebellion; he saw destiny kindle within her. They had no plan, only an identity, a tacit creed they shared like a dim and fragile flame in the night.

Sometimes, that is enough.

And that is when Njegwe learned an important lesson:

Even in exile, the roots are deep, and the forests, those ancient holders of stories wait alive, patiently able to become again.

Chapter 7: Whispers in the Camp

The night came down gently upon the camp, enveloping the flimsy coverings in shadow. In the torn fabric shell of their tiny shelter, the air was heavy with unspoken stress, weighed down by days stacked with fear and anxiety. Njegwe and Catalina sat side by side, shoulders touching, sharing a moment of calm amid the chaos. Shadows spasmed on the weathered canvas, created by an unstable lantern or perhaps their own uneasy thoughts. Outside, the distant whisper of guards' footfalls and indistinct murmurs from other detainees wove a haunting symphony of hopelessness, a reminder of the invisible walls that encased them.

They had been pinching bits of time over days, murmuring quiet words and casting long looks that spoke of possibility without saying it. Their hands had brushed as they passed by, all silent, yet pleased with this tormenting life of subjugation and the ruins of the past. Tonight, they learned from each other, realizing that their fate depended on the courage and determination of two people, and on the slender reed of hope to which they clung.

"I cannot remain here," Catalina murmured, her voice trembling, charged with both fear and stubborn resolution. "They will return me, and I won't go."

Njegwe nodded, frowning in comprehension. His eyes shone in the flickering lantern as he glanced around them. "They took our names, our stories. But we are more than just numbers. We must find a way out. We must try."

Her gaze was smooth as a river-stone, steady, with emotions coursing through it.

"How? They watch us all the time. The guards are everywhere. And the fences, they're high, wired, and hard to climb."

Njegwe reached for his pocket, his fingers shaking lightly as he pulled out a ragged piece of cloth, a flimsy old remnant of life before, the last gift his mother had given him. The material was worn but cherished, a physical reminder of home. "We must find a weak link somewhere," he muttered to himself. "A crack in the system. Something they forget about, or an instant when their guard is down. We must be patient, observant."

Catalina gave the matter some thought before nodding. "We could wait for the guard change," she offered. "Perhaps no one will notice us then. But we need a plan. Something precise. Something that doesn't allow for errors."

They studied their scant pool of possibilities, exchanged stories of escapes they'd heard about from back home, accounts of resilience and cunning passed from detainee to detainee, whispers of hope in the face of despair. Occasionally, the faraway scrape of a guardsman's boots or cries from the watchtower reminded them of what was at stake. Yet they spoke quietly, and with every word exchanged, their determination grew stronger.

"I still remember the forest near my village," Njegwe murmured, eyes distant. "The trees taught me patience. If you listen long enough, they whisper secrets. Maybe the camp has its own whispers, hidden paths, overlooked gaps, areas where the guards aren't looking."

Catalina smiled slightly, eyes shining with soft hope. "In Guatemala, we say that the river knows the way. If we let it take us, maybe it carries us as far away from it as the current that brings us back home, no matter how distant we are."

Their mutual suffering, the deprivation of their homes, the shattering unfairness of forced emigration, and the uncertainty about what lay ahead outweighed not knowing each other's language. In private hours, they embraced the shared stories of each other, acknowledging that their trauma belonged to a larger tapestry of displacement and resilience. In their shared agony, they established an unspoken solidarity, a mutual agreement not to allow despair to devour them.

They readied their improvised tools: bits of wire, a small piece of broken metal, some rags, things that could possibly help if the need arose. They schemed, they murmured reassurances, and made all their movements slow and silent, deliberately so as not to draw attention.

"We'll bide our time," Njegwe murmured, voice barely a breeze. "And when it comes, we run. We are racing toward the forest, toward the river, to all those stories that called us across distance, from a place least like death and most like life.

Then Catalina put forth her hand, trembling with fearful resolve. "Together," she murmured, cementing their silent promise.

The camp seemed to listen in the dark, as if holding its breath. The night bore whispers of secrets, for those who would listen, and for those who would dream of freedom. Somewhere out there, beyond the fences, was their future, lurking in the darkness, waiting for an opportunity to escape the bonds of fear and hopelessness.

They sat together in silence, the rustling of the wind in the trees echoing their determination: they would not break. They would return to the forests, the rivers, and the stories that restored their spirits.

Chapter 8: The Forest of Becoming

They sneaked out of the woods like whispers, barely visible, as if darkness itself had conspired to cover them.

The sentries had already fallen asleep, tired out by their own insensitivity and false sense of security, and a faint snore emanated from the gates of the encampment. Some guards became aware of their disappearance and tracked the fugitives' footsteps with a team of K-9 dogs. Nearly two hours later, Catalina stopped running; the guards were far too near. Njegwe had heard a story from one of his maternal granduncles about how they outran the French colonial army in Cameroon. He took off Catalina's shoes and repaired them. He also fixed his own. When they opted to go south, their footprints indicated they were currently heading north.

During the war against the nationalists and Bamiléké populations of western Cameroon, "maquisards" (nationalist fighters) and villagers devised multiple methods to hide out and disguise themselves to avoid detection by French colonial forces on assignment alongside Cameroonian allies. They wore their shoes backward to create a ruse of footprints that led soldiers astray. That method, recounted by his granduncle, had saved their lives.

And the moon, always the silent co-plotter of any escape drama ever told, threw down silvery fingers through the dense foliage, lending its shy, trembling light to outline the tangle of underbrush. It was as though the night itself welcomed their flight, showing them the way with hushed, elder knowing.

Barefoot and fierce, Catalina let herself be pulled forward in time with the pace of the trees, each step an act of will and belief. Moonlight flickered in her river-stone eyes, and they flashed with determination.

"Nearly there."

Njegwe nodded, dropping the weight of captivity an ounce at a time with each dry shake of leaves against their feet, in cadence with the chorus of faith ringing in their ears.

The forest was far from typical. It throbbed with the sound of muting accessory magic in its echoing heart, a thing ancient and immune to borders, wars, or walls. Vines looped themselves into question marks around ancient limbs, telling secrets known only to the woods. Fireflies blinked in rhythmic cipher, their minuscule bodies flickering a language older than words, messages sent heavenward, or perhaps backward; signals of hope, warning, or merely the recording of events past. The air was heavy with the smell of moss, sod, and memory; each breath reminded them not so much of their own lives as of those that came before.

Somewhere nearby, a jaguar growled softly, not in threat, but in acknowledgment, guardian of this otherworldly era.

"It was a guttural sound in the silence we both heard," they said. It clearly defined their presence and the reason for their being there. They followed it for what seemed like hours, possibly days, lost in the solace of the canopy, sunlight providing such complete shelter that time stretched around them.

At night, they slept under the dense canopy of towering ceiba trees, whose roots groped deep into the soil, ancestral arms reaching for someone to hold. In hushed tones, she told him tales of Catalina, the goddess of the moon who watched over those driven from their homes, and of forest spirits that protected the dreams of people looking for a safe place to settle. Her voice was a lullaby of leaves and stars, soft, but heavy with the weight of all that lived to see eternity. He listened, not with his ears, but as someone for whom the pain of remembering how to believe in magic, in possibility, and in himself had been too great.

After a while, the forest grew hauntingly quiet.

The roads that had yawned open to them doubled back as riddles. The birds fell silent, their songs swallowed by an eerie hush. It smelled of nothing, made no promise other than emptiness. They were lost and hungry, and hope itself was a thin, shining knife, cutting through the moonlight that dribbled through cracks in the leaves. Then the girl with the river-stone eyes began to question the forest's hold, her belief flickering like a guttering flame. So did Njegwe, his confidence waning as he second-guessed himself.

One night, he left her and slipped into the shadows of the forest, feeling lost and searching for a sign, something to show him the way, some measure of right and wrong. The moon hung high, casting a cold, silver light through the interlaced boughs. As he passed, the trees seemed to glisten with a peculiar, otherworldly glow. In the very shadow, he saw a viper with horns, which, in the Bamileke ethnic group of Western Cameroon, symbolized twin babies, mysterious yet bringing good luck. He began to monologue, pondering the significance of what had just happened.

He kept walking and soon found himself in a clearing he hadn't noticed before: a perfect circle, peaceful and disturbingly silent. Faceted stones lay in a spiral, glimmering softly and buzzing with subdued power. On a throne hewn of bark and bone sat a figure cloaked in shadow and gold, an ancient man or king, regal yet ghostly, the very image of authority stretched across eternity.

His face was strikingly familiar, though not from memory, but from blood, from lineage. His eyes held the age of centuries, and when he spoke, his voice was like thunder cloaked in silk – booming and deep.

"You bear my name," the figure boomed, the sound reverberating through the clearing. "You carry my exile."

Njegwe went to his knees, panting. "Who are you?" he managed to whisper.

"I am the one on whom you were born. A king, yes, but only in part. A keeper of stories. A builder of sanctuary." The king's eyes seemed to bore into him. "You are not lost, child. You are being tested."

The forest around them seemed to draw back, living and waiting. The circle of rocks glowed from within, casting a warm light into the darkness.

"But to survive in this place," the king continued, "you must not listen with your ears, but with your bones. The forest does not simply give. It must be courted. It demands honesty. Offer it your truth."

Njegwe's voice shook. "But I don't have anything."

At length, the king staggered to his feet and rested a heavy, kindly hand upon his shoulder. "Then give it your emptiness. Let it fill you."

A staff was offered to him, inlaid with symbols, one from his Cameroonian ancestry, and the other from Mayan legend. "This will guide you," the king whispered. “Not through the forest, but through yourself.”

Njegwe felt a deep recognition stir within him, as though the figure before him had walked from the same dreams he had long cherished in Cameroon, visions of his great-grandfather.

In an instant, the clearing vanished, the spirals disappeared, and the light faded to nothing. He stood alone, his staff in one hand, trembling, yet somehow more at peace, more grounded.

And when he came back to Catalina, the change was apparent. Her voice was softer, yet questioning. "You found something."

He offered a faint smile. "No," he said quietly. "Something found me."

From that day, the forest seemed reborn. Roads stretched out like ribbons of light. The birds returned, singing the songs of rebirth. A babbling icy stream flowed with intent, purifying and curative. They bathed in it, washing away the grime of captivity and the scars of exile. She wove leaves and feathers into his hair, each knot a prayer. He studied the ridges of her palm, reading an unspoken map for a future they could not yet imagine.

And then, one night, the forest opened its voice, a chorus of life and promise once more.

A column of quetzals marched overhead, their emerald tails streaking out behind them like flags of hope. On the breeze came the warm smell of cacao and copal, sparking memories of home. Far off, a gleam of golden, welcoming light shone, human in its warmth.

They stared at each other, both horrified and in awe. "Are we ready?" he asked softly.

She squeezed his hand, her voice steadier and stronger than he'd ever heard it. "We are becoming."

And now, with the forest at their backs and the unknown ahead, they no longer lurched into the future as fugitives of exile, but as seeds of resilience, ready to yield whole new stories and write new beginnings.

Chapter 9: The Samaritan

The village danced like a mirage, tumbling at the edge of his sight.

It lay between two ancient hills, shrouded in a tenuous veil of morning mist. Perhaps it was less a place than something men had whispered into being, half-remembered and spoken into subtlety. The air was cool and moist, sweet with the earth and blooming flowers, yet laced with the faint tang of woodsmoke that drifted from some distant chimney. Silence was pressed, countered only by the distant, faint chorus of children playing, briefly drifting in the breeze in an odd way that made everything seem so delicate yet unbreakable.

As they drew closer, the mist thickened around them, wrapping them in a crawling cauldron of white and grey. The grave dirt beneath their feet, once stretching to meet across the clearing, had become a tangled mass of roots and leaves, as though the earth itself were struggling in vain for a secret it could not bear. Each footstep felt unsure, muffled by moss and fallen petals, the world around them seeming to hold its breath.

But they were not alone.

From the fog emerged a figure, neither hostile nor friendly, but present, as if the forest had materialized him from within. He was tall and stout, dressed in a woven robe made of banana plant fibers interwoven with feathers, softly aglow in the muted light.

His eyes, void and whirling like storm clouds looming over the horizon after rain, bore the silence of untold centuries. In one hand, he held a lantern glowing amber, casting warm pools of light that danced as though each were a tiny star. In the other, he carried a small pouch that jingled faintly with seeds and stones, tokens of stories and memories he held close.

"You've travelled a long way," he whispered, his voice murmuring like the wind, words as sweet as song.

"As much as I feel a chill, that isn't the word. I am a living soul, not a ghost," Catalina said, her voice calm as though warmth had returned to her bones. "Too far to turn back."

He nodded slowly, as if weighing her words, and then gestured gently with a beckoning hand, urging her toward him.

Noiselessly, they followed, moving farther and deeper into the mist-clouded woods, their steps soundless upon the damp earth carpeted with fallen leaves. The silence was not intimidating or oppressive; it felt sacred, purposeful. The trees around them grew taller, their branches spread like arms yearning toward the sky, whispering ancient tales they could almost make out.

Then the woods opened into an unfamiliar clearing, a sanctuary that seemed born from the wild imagination of the earth itself. It was a garden, but not one shaped by human hands. There were no straight rows or manicured lawns. Instead, wild herbs bent into spirals, their leaves curving into question marks and signs of forgotten mysteries. Fruit trees leaned toward one another, branches entwined as if two lovers were sharing a secret. Vines hugged the air, thick with flowers and ripe fruit, murmuring tales of blossoming, patience, and fortitude.

At the center stood a little cabin, simple yet powerful in its simplicity. Its walls were adorned with symbols from across the world: Mayan glyphs glowing as though reflecting ancient rainforests, Adinkra's starbursts from Africa radiating wisdom and hope, and graceful Arabic calligraphy floating like a poem in the air. It was a place that not only crossed borders, but also ideas and memories.

"This is a place for outsiders," he said, his voice merging with the rustling leaves.

Catlina lifted her pretty head and searched for him, her eyes full of quiet defiance. "Then we belong here," she said, her voice trembling slightly but free of doubt.

For a long moment, he regarded them with a heavy gaze filled with understanding and regret. Then, with a single nod, he motioned for them to enter.

Inside, the sanctuary pulsed with warmth. He offered them food: cassava cakes, roasted plantains, and a fragrant brown tea brewed from forest leaves. Earthy and rich, it tasted like memory itself. As they ate, he began to tell stories of those who had once passed through this sacred place.

Of an Ethiopian priest who fled war, whose prayers had sown seeds of hope in the soil.

Of a Haitian healer fleeing persecution, whose herbs and chants had woven healing into the warp and weft of the garden.

Of a Salvadoran poet who had lost her voice in the camps, yet whose words lingered in the leaves and stones, waiting to be reclaimed.

Each story was a seed, a prayer grown and planted in the sanctuary's soil. The garden had consumed them, weaving their spirits into its roots.

"You will leave something behind," he murmured quietly, his voice like a breeze rustling through leaves.

"We have nothing," she whispered, her voice thick with hopelessness.

He shook his head, smiling sadly. "You have everything. You have your story."

They spent the night in the hut, encircled by runes and whispers. Their sleep was restless, filled with shifting shapes, glimpses of runes etched in stone, chants beneath starlit skies, and the spirits of their forebears standing guard.

Once more, the vision of the old king came to the Cameroonian, sowing seeds into rich, dark soil, his grim lips mouthing ancient words over the earth. His hands moved like the wind, signaling hope for the days ahead.

Catalina dreamed of a tall ceiba tree that grew inside her chest, sending shoots upward and branches stretching toward the stars, carrying her desires and memories beyond the confines of exile.

"I have a gift for your coming journey," he said the next morning, handing them a piece of bark carved with symbols, a map not inked on paper but etched into the wood itself.

"Keep to the wind," he whispered faintly. "It knows the way better than any compass. Trust it."

"Will we see you again?" Njegwe asked hesitantly.

He smiled, a gentle, knowing smile. "Not unless you get lost," he replied.

Then he disappeared into the mist. Only his voice lingered, its echo hanging for a moment longer until all that was left was its receding memory, whispering softly with the promise that he would watch over Catalina.

That was her only goodbye.

They left the sanctuary, their hearts heavy and yet somehow hopeful. The forest embraced them once more, its paths unfurling like petals murmuring secrets. Every step they took felt weighted, memories in one hand and hopes in the other. Somewhere ahead, in the Village of Forgotten Names, lay not just recognition but remembrance. There, they would dwell perpetually in their stories, drifting and settling in quiet backwaters of belonging.

And so they went, lit by the morning's inner glow, carrying in their hearts a piece of the sacred garden, a flicker of hope, a nucleus of belongings waiting to unfold in the world beyond.

Chapter 10: The Village of Forgotten Names

The forest parted like a veil, revealing a secret world beneath its embrace.

The mist cleared slowly around the last bend in the path, as though hesitant to reveal what lay hidden. Little by little, the fog pulled back, revealing a rich valley nestled between emerald hills that rose and fell like titans sleeping in the light of dawn. The land spread before them in silent glory, green, teeming, alive, murmuring secrets borne by the wind.

Clusters of wooden huts with rounded peaks like turtles' backs were scattered across the valley, gathered in thatched-roofed circles along its slopes. Smoke curled upwards from open cook fires, floating idly into the radiant sky, carrying with it the scent of roasting maize, rain-soaked earth, and something older still, a sacred, indivisible memory woven into the air itself. It was a perfume of roots reaching deep into history. It smelled of endurance, of inherited stories.

Njegwe stopped at the edge of the clearing, feeling as if his eyes might pop out and his heart might burst open, spilling all it had experienced: border crossings, detention camps, enchanted woods, and conversations with kings buried under centuries of dust. But nothing in his travels had prepared him for this place.

This quiet hamlet in the heart of Guatemala felt more foreign than any checkpoint or prison gate, not because it had been unusual in shape or fragrance, but simply because it hadn't demanded anything from him. It just sat there, waiting. Patient.

As if it had always known he would arrive, if only his name could balance on a fragile strip of paper.

The air felt still, catching in his chest as he took it all in, the pulse of life that beat quietly below the surface.

At his side, the girl with river-stone eyes, whose name he now understood was Catalina, placed her hand gently in his. Her touch was steady, grounding. She spoke softly, but with unwavering truth. "They're not going to ask who you are," she said. "They'll ask what you carry."

The significance of her words hung heavy in the room. It was a reminder that, in this place, who you were mattered less than what you carried, your stories and scars, your hopes and promises.

There they entered the village and passed through the gate of the still city.

Barefoot children whirled past them, laughter ringing along the winding paths. Their play, clapping, chasing, and hiding, beat like a living heart of joy within the valley. Elders with weathered yet luminous faces shuffled under woven awnings, grinding dried corn kernels in textile-processed hands. Nearby, a packet with colored cloth lay open, images transforming into symbols and legends. Nobody gawked, nobody questioned why they were there. But Njegwe saw recognition in their eyes, the silent acknowledgment of shared history and collective resilience.

A woman came up to them first. Her silver-threaded hair flowed like moonlight, and her dark eyes were keen and watchful as black glass. She was wearing a huipil embroidered with jaguars stalking through stars, symbols of power and mystery.

"You've come out of the forest," she said, her voice clear and soft.

Njegwe nodded silently.

"Then you've been tested," she replied, both affirmation and challenge.

She took them along a narrow path that ran in and out of the village until they reached a small hut close by the river. Its walls were painted with spirals, blazing suns, and ancestral figures dancing through cycles of rebirth and eternal connection.

"This is yours now," she murmured as he neared her from behind. "Not that you deserve it, but because you need it."

Her voice carried the weight of understanding, of knowing what it meant to be scattered and yet still rooted in hope.

Inside, the hut was spare: a woven mat on the earthen floor, a clay jug, a bundle of healing herbs, and sacred objects that whispered of protection and memory. It was modest, yet filled with a holy silence, as though centuries had folded themselves gently into its walls.

A single flame flickered in the corner, seeming to breathe in and out, as if exhaling all the stories of all who had ever passed before them.

Then came the drums. Not perfectly in rhythm, but pulsing from memory itself, like the beat of ancestral blood calling spirits and waking histories. Catalina danced on her feet, her twirls drawing forms older than words, her body undulating in harmony with whatever stirred within the darkness.

Njegwe watched, tension tightening in his chest. Then slowly, inch by trembling inch, he looked at her and forced himself forward. He felt the weight of centuries in the villager's silent gaze. They were not listening with their ears. They were listening with their hearts. With their spirits.

After Catalina's dance, the silver-haired woman stood and addressed them, her voice carrying both power and compassion.

"Do not speak our names here," she whispered, her words flowing like a holy prayer. "We are called by what we survive. We are named by what we create."

Her eyes shifted to Njegwe, sharp but kind. "You are not Cameroonian here. You are not an exile. You are a seed."

Her words settled like dew into the night. "And seeds," she continued softly, "have to be planted."

The villagers came forward bearing gifts, not gold or coin, but tools, each one representing a promise of a fresh start. A machete honed with purpose, a woven basket full of hope, a flute carved from bone and wood, ready to carry their stories forward. Each gift was a seed. An offering of strength, resilience, and renewal.

Njegwe slept that night with the gentle murmur of the river in his ears and the smell of maize haunting the wind. His dreams collected visions of bridges woven from vines that connected the world. He saw lions and quetzals seated together upon a mountain throne. He saw a village where no name was lost, only reborn, like the seasons changing.

He woke at dawn no longer feeling like a refugee wandering through loss, but like a root buried deep in the wisdom of the earth, ready to rise. The sanctified place had absorbed him not as a stranger, but as part of a living tale that stretched beyond borders, beyond walls, into the vast terrain of memory and aspiration.

He kept his eyes fixed on the new sun rising over their village. It made him feel like a man who belonged to stories, a vessel of fortitude and song, a seed that would grow into something bigger than the ground from which it emerged.

Chapter 11: Seeds of Trust

Njegwe never failed to rise with the first ray of dawn, when clouds cringed beneath the edges of an amber sun. The river that ran past his humble hut sang its morning hymn, notes winding as if they were whispers of remembered spirits rising. The village, still in the sweet cradle of sleep, stirred gently as feathers moved, grinding stones turning against slabs, murmured greetings spoken in a language older than written words. It was a rhythm steeped in patience and reverence, one that moved in unison with the rising sun. Shoeless, he stepped out the door and felt the cool earth beneath his soles, the grains of soil, patches of moss, scattered stones pressing against his skin like unspoken prayers. For years, he had awakened every day with fear tightening its grip around his chest. Here, in this quiet village among rolling hills, a different feeling began to take root. This peace was not passive. It had been earned, step by step, through trust.

Resting beside the doorway was the machete that had been given to him the day before, sparkling with a soft gleam in the early morning light. It no longer felt like a weapon, but a tool for survival. Njegwe brushed his hand gently over the handle and felt a silent force course through his grip.

He trudged to the fields, where villagers crouched over rows of maize and beans, their bodies swaying with the wind like the crops they tended.

No one beckoned him. No one instructed him. But Njegwe was seen by a woman with a face marked by many stories whose eyes were sharp as obsidian but softened with kindness. She was old, her body broken, but her spirit untouched. As he knelt beside her, fastidiously pulling weeds from the ground, she looked at him and smiled, not one of approval or condescension, but recognition; that kind of understanding words could not convey.

"You work like someone who has lost something," she murmured, her voice like dry leaves shifting in the wind.

Njegwe stilled. A shadow briefly passed behind his eyes.

She nodded, her gaze steady. "Then you'll know how to safeguard whatever you've discovered." That reminds Njegwe, word by word, of what his late granduncle used to tell him. He felt like it was the déjà entendu. He briefly considered the possibility that his granduncle may have reincarnated into another body. He also thought of the poem of Birago Diop stating that: "Those who die are never gone:

They're in the shadows that get brighter

And in the shadows that get darker

They're in the trembling trees

They're in the howling woods

They're in the calm streams..."

Days stretched into weeks. Njegwe worked in silence, each movement a quiet prayer, each chore one more step toward gaining trust. His hands grew rough with calluses, yet remained careful and deliberate, learning the language of the earth and sky.

He patched roofs that sheltered families from the rain, fetched river water in clay jugs, and collected firewood under the relentless heat of the sun. Every act was a seed planted in the community's fruitful soil, an act of giving, one of belonging.

He listened more than he spoke. Stories were not told through questions, but over cooking fires, in quiet moments of work, and in soft exchanges of daily life.

An old man, his voice gravelly yet sweet with nostalgia, talked about running away from the mountains during the civil war, holding on to nothing more than a flute and prayer, hope his only treasure. One woman described how her family had disappeared in the violence, but she had only one heirloom to show for it: a clay pot that never cracked, no matter how fiercely it was fired, a symbol of resilience and continuity. Each story settled within Njegwe's heart like a seed, blossoming gradually into understanding. Into trust.

Catalina observed him intently, his eyes flickering like the cool current of the river that ran through their village. She understood now that he was not an alien, but a scholar, one who wished to know the speech of the country and its inhabitants. She began to help him understand the names of plants growing in the fields: chaya with its vivid leaves, red chilies, and even the healing properties of aloe. Njegwe remembered very well the bitterness of the Aloe, because he and his siblings were forced to take it during every corn season when growing up. She taught him the symbols woven into the women's huipils, jaguar claws for strength, stars for guidance, and "the spiral of life." Then she sang him songs that had the music of rain and the pulse of the earth.

In exchange, Njegwe would tell stories from his country: Cameroon's sacred rituals and elders who whispered wisdom beneath the forest cover, and lion dances in honor of the kings and ancestors that kept the spirits alive. He talked about forest elders who knew the secret paths, rituals that summoned rain, and dances that wove community and memory into movement.

One evening, as the sun sank behind the hills and stretched long shadows across the mountain path, they gathered around him, wide-eyed and restless with anticipation. They pulled at his sleeves and pleaded, "Tell us a story from your country."

He paused, then sighed. The words flowed slowly at first, then picked up speed. "Once," he began, "there was a boy born in a palace, but he never seemed like a prince. He wandered, and he lost his name, only to find it again in a land where no one could understand his tongue. He discovered that kings are not anointed with blood, but by service, by listening, by standing beside others, by lifting those who cannot rise alone." The children listened, spellbound, their eyes sparkling as if the stars were near friends.

"Was the boy you?" one inquired, awe quivering in his voice.

Njegwe smiled softly. "He's becoming me," he answered.

That night, when the silver-haired elder of the village approached him once more. Her eyes reflected nothing but understanding. She spoke softly and with determination. "You've planted something here," she whispered. "Not just crops. But trust."

"It's going to grow," she continued, "only if you stay."

Njegwe looked up at the sky, his hand resting on the old king's staff, carved with symbols carved into its wood, reminders of an old life and a future hope. He recalled the circle of stones in the woods, the king's whispers, and the silent promise of that staff. His exile had left scars, but here under the dome of this endless sky, he felt a new tug, an ancient summons to belong, to embed himself in this resilient earth.

"I'm going to stay," he said, softly but firmly. "Not because I must. But because I choose to."

At that instant, the Village of Forgotten Names did not remember Njegwe as the exile, but as Njegwe the seed, embryonic and capable of offering hope once it took root.

He felt the sun's heat climb higher and light a new chapter, grown out of faithfulness, of sacred planting after the roots had been pulled up. And in his heart, he understood this was the start of something eternal. Something unbreakable.

Chapter 12: Nostalgia and Nightmares

The rain came suddenly, a torrent that washed through the village with the force of long-buried memories. Heavy drops fell from the sky in an outpouring of stories, drenching the earth and releasing the scent of mangoes ripening beneath the sun, of moist red clay baked by afternoon heat, of woodsmoke curling from fires back home.

The villagers welcomed it with open arms. Laughter rose above the patter of rain. Voices lifting into song. Feet splashed through puddles. They danced barefoot, their arms aloft to the very sky, as though yielding themselves to the sacred rhythm of renewal poured from the heavens.

But Njegwe stood apart beneath the towering ceiba tree, its trunk rising like a silent sentinel. His eyes were shut as if he were praying with all his heart. For him, the rain was a ghost from his past, the memory of something that haunted him with every falling drop. It was a taste of home, from a country where every storm bore the voice of his ancestors and every raindrop was an offering to the spirits.

That night, the nightmares returned.

Dark, twisting visions thrust him into a spiraling web of pain and memory. Once again, he saw the detention camp, with its steel doors clanging and flickering lights that cast shadows on the cold concrete. He listened to the pounding of headless soldiers' feet, their unrecognizable words shouting out in orders. Shackles clanged, icy and unforgiving. The words "Case 47-B" echoed through his thoughts like a dark curse, the number that had killed him and made him what he was.

But then, the dream shifted.

He was home in Cameroon, standing before his father's throne, a seat of honor and power. The elders had joined him, their faces obscured by whirling smoke. His father spoke, his hand outstretched, but Njegwe was paralyzed in place. Cold, foreign earth squelched around his feet. The throne upon which he sat fell beneath him, dissolving into dust, and the lively village that lay before them turned to nothing more than a pile of ash and silence.

He awoke so suddenly that the entire bed shook, cold sweat dripping down his forehead.

Catalina was there in a moment, her warm hands firm on his shoulders as she murmured softly in his ear, "You were dreaming in another language."

He sat up, hand over his heart, eyes flashing with unspoken hurt, "I was thinking of home," he confessed, his voice shaking with emotion.

She turned her eyes on him, tender and insistent. "Is this not home?" she asked softly.

He didn't answer immediately. Instead, he looked at the early light of daybreak and reached for words that could outweigh, stand up to, the weight in his heart.

The next day, looking for answers, Njegwe roamed to the end of the village, where the forest called out once again, a dark, knotted frontier between worlds.

He settled under a venerable tree, whose scarred bark twisted like the hands of a storyteller. He sat cross-legged on the yielding ground and turned his head to the wind as he spoke. H He wasn't talking to anyone at all, but rather to the air itself. It was as if he was calling down to the spirits of his ancestors, dead forebears, or even just trying to send a message back home.

"I miss you, Cameroon," he whispered, like a lover longing. "Your music, your colors, your chaos. I miss being recognized by my name, by my people, by my land."

Then, as if in answer to his longing, the memories rushed on like an avalanche of sights and smells.

He was back in the courtyard of his youth, golden patterns shimmering in the sunlight across the red earth. His mother's voice filled the air, reaching him as she crushed the Taro in the wooden mortar and beat it with her pestle. The scent of yellow soup filled the kitchen, rich, spicy, and fragrant, as the laughter of children echoed between the walls, chasing each other around the mango trees, their voices lifting to swell like the chorus of innocence.

He recalled the market sellers calling out, an abundance of woven baskets overflowing with colorful fruits and vegetables, drums setting a beat, and even the elders swaying to the rhythm. He remembered the warm, sudden rain in Dje, it is warm and sudden-smelling rain that washes the dust from the streets and fills puddles like mirrors of the storm-dark sky.

He remembered the way the earth felt between his fingers as he helped his mother plant cassava and beans. He recalled her stories by firelight, each ending with a proverb that lingered like a refrain in a greater song:

“For whom did not know where the rain began to beat him could not say where he dried.”

He remembered his language, l aced with rhythm and time. Every word carried the weight of those who came before him. And every phrase is a fiber weaving them all together. He had belonged, not just to land, but to people, to cadence, to meaning. Here in this foreign country, Njegwe could feel himself fading, like a photograph left too long in the sun, still visible but no longer clear.

“Whole,” he murmured to the wind. “Here, I am learning to be whole again.”

The wind answered him not in words, but with a soft whisper in the trees, as if it took them to the place he meant. A single feather fell from the sky, landing softly across his lap. It was like a quetzal feather, resplendent in emerald and green, sacred and alive with history. He took it, grasping it tenderly, warmth spreading through his fingers.

He took it as a sign.

Later, he tramped to the village’s shrine, a holy ground where offerings were left for ancestors and spirits to honor, to remember, and to seek guidance. He set the quetzal feather next to a carved lion, a talisman of strength and protection he’d chiseled himself. Then he knelt, his knees bent, and softly crept, his voice trembling, scarcely as he wept.

"I am not forgetting you. I am turning into you, somewhere else.”

There, he met the silver-haired woman, who had been waiting for him, calm and all-knowing.

"You are grieving," she said.

“Yes,” Njegwe confessed, his voice thick with concern.

"Good," she replied softly. "Grief is a bridge. Cross it slowly."

That night, his dreams returned. But this time, the forest was quiet, and the spirits were kind. His father wasn't seated on a throne, but next to a soft fire, dancing flames pulsating like the heartbeat of a home from afar. The old man gave Njegwe a tiny seed, humble in appearance but filled with potential.

“Plant this where they’ll know you’ve been here,” he added softly. “Not where they know you, but where your roots can grow.”

Njegwe woke with tears on his face, not heavy tears of despair, but cleansing, like rain washing dust from stone.

He stepped onto the street and looked down toward the edge of the village, not at the strangers, but at the roots. Deep, intricate systems woven under the soil, steadying him in the earth’s arms.

And in that instant, a quiet peace took root within him, nostalgia no longer an ache, but a bloom.

He understood now.

This was his soil, his story built in the fibers of this place, as sacred as the rain, powerful as the wind. And there, in the silence before dawn, he caught a glimpse of redemption’s hope, an ancestral song echoed in a new melody.

Chapter 13: The Circle of Hands

The sun was low, throwing a warm amber light across the village and giving everything that soft warmth that dulled the hard edges of day.

In the middle of the clearing, Njegwe stood calm and sure in front of all the villagers who had gathered. They'd welcomed him as a stranger, an exile, a wanderer from faraway lands, but today he came to plant something more profound: the seeds of a new system based on mutual trust, drawn from his Cameroonian background and shaped by the strength and shared humanity of this diverse group.

The villagers gathered in a wide, loose circle around a gasping fire whose wavering light cast small, pale pools of brightness on their faces, and the lines of hardship and hope had been graven into them, too. People had come here from chaos, and those stories were knitted into the cloth of their faces in their expressions and in the lights still present in the eyes that had witnessed too much. Desperation hung heavily in the air, but so did anticipation, and a tender hope that only needed a spark to ignite.

Njegwe took a slow, measured breath and looked around him, the pulse of life taking over, beating hearts in unison, stories echoing from the walls. And then he extended his palms, it was a gesture of peace and offering, and spoke in his voice, a calm and steady voice, "From my village..." he began quietly, "we say that with Nsie (God), your roots are strongest when they intermingle instead of seeking to strangle one another; the giants do not strike down competition or other branches we grow together." He looked out over the crowd and met each elder, woman, and child's eyes, one by one, as if they were all an important part of this moment. "When one tree falls, others can take cover under its leaves, and when roots are bound deep enough in the earth, no storm, no wind, can pull us out of the ground."

Here he paused, letting his words settle like seeds in fertile soil, then continued with a soft smile: "And I want to thank you for taking me in, for opening your hearts ... as the world turned its back. Even as I was wrongfully deported from the country that I loved, you proved that community is not defined by borders or laws but by love, shared stories, and humanity."

Then, holding out a tiny woven bracelet, Njegwe went on: "This is a symbol of hands in a circle; it tells us that our strength is rooted in one another, that we flourish through mutual aid. We all have skills, stories, and resources. And when we share them, we create a community of strength and resilience that's made up not only of mighty trees but also the thousands of scratches that, millions of blades that form an unbreakable forest.

His hands raised the meaning of the gesture, which was quickly passed from one to another, just as the movement defining Cameroonian dance in a continuous line, everyone and everything from one to the whole, a single fluid muscle unity in motion.

"We can build, here, what is called by some Tequio, or collective work for the common good. And everybody puts in what they can, whether it's work or knowledge, and then we all grow." His voice was soft, but there was an underlying firmness to it that beat like a heartbeat, drumming out a steady rhythm in support of their collective cause.

He paused again, dipped his hand into one bag, and produced a group of small amulets: seeds, stones, and a carved piece of wood representing an ancestor's face. "These are symbols," he said quietly, "a seed to plant hope; a stone to make us remember our strength; and the face of an ancestor that is reminding us of our roots. They are gifts and obligations. To protect, nurture, and remember."

At first, the villagers were hesitant; they had never seen these strange signs from an outsider, but Njegwe was steady and pure in his intentions and won them over. They formed a circle, one by one, passing the tokens to each other as they shared stories of hardship, perseverance, and hope. Each one vowed to help; the unspoken pledge from now on, as a ring of roots grew up around them.

Catalina looked on in silent understanding, her eyes glowing with gratitude. "In Guatemala," she whispered, "we call this Tequio, but it's also B'eleje collective effort. Today we make our own b'eleje, a circle that elevates everyone, one that binds us in strength and faith."

Njegwe winced as the force and the heat of their common spirit hit her. "As an outsider," he whispered, "I offer no land or title. But I bring my skills, my traditions, and my belief that community is a living thing, what we grow and feed every day. But I think we can even learn from one another. My roots are in Cameroon, and the respect I have for you and your culture will help us build our future on hard work, cooperation, and mutual respect. In Cameroon, we love people no matter their skin color, their religion, or their origin. We did not love people like a wealthy person loves his wealth; we did not love people like a gold owner loves his gold. We love people because they are people like us."

In subsequent days, Njegwe began to incorporate his own practices rooted in his heritage: communal planting, group decision-making, and storytelling circles in which elders and children are honored. He incorporated patterns from Cameroonian textiles and movements from ancestral dances into the village's routines.

He set up storytelling sessions where elders shared stories of resilience, skills such as weaving, cooking, and farming. This was a collaborative effort to trade off skills with each other, an exercise meant to build trust, based on a Bamileke tradition called *Nsuck*, which is the fact that this week, people will gather together to help one or more persons, and the following week, it will be some people or someone’s turn.

Njegwe was the kind of leader who took things gently, a strong but not forceful invitation, like planting a seed and waiting. He applied his cultural skills to foster the sense that people had agency, knew their capacity to be authors of their collective future and builders of destiny, just as all actions were bound by the strength of shared roots.

One evening, as they sat by the fire, Njegwe raised his hands again and spoke with conviction. "In my country," he murmured, "we say that the roots of a tree are in the ground, hidden but just as important. Today, I see how deep and tangled its roots are, binding us in trust and power. We’re not just survivors; we’re building a new family.”

The villagers nodded, smiled, and clapped quietly, realizing his words paved a way to connect past pain, bringing hope for the future. They knew they could not waste a single moment that Njegwe was with them, a treasure to be unwrapped and savored, because, even as an outsider, he had helped them make something new together, something built on mutual aid, cultural exchange, and the unbreakable cords of shared commitment.

His eyes shut for a moment, then he said quietly, "Thank you for protecting me, for considering me one of your own even when I wasn't home and the world thought I was gone. Your kindness is a beacon. I vow to keep this promise by supporting us with one glass of wine at a time as we grow old together."

Into the night as it grew later, the circle of hands remained unbroken, a record of determination. The fire crackled in the darkness of an evening, throwing half-lit shadows onto the stars above, like silent spectators, sentinels to a world reborn; fortified by human design and trust forged from conviction, thriving not only out of necessity but on deep-rooted ties that grew in the soil of their humankind.

Chapter 14: Quetzals and Lions

The sun was setting, and the sky had turned orange and violet. Music and laughter mingled in the village square, rippling out into the muggy night air like a living pulse. Lanterns fluttered on the fringe of the throng, sending shafts of golden light onto the villagers' faces, lit with joyous expectation. Tonight wasn't just a celebration, but the beautiful polymerization that I have had the great privilege of watching over all these joyous years, worlds and traditions long carried, woven with new threads being told that will one day bring light to later nights around them.

It was Catalina, with her river-stone eyes and long, soft smile. It was the rhythms of drumming she had absorbed from Cameroon, translated into her dance, a new kind of confidence running through it. Her body swayed to the rhythm and her footsteps, in syncopation with the b'eleje, all at once. With her ancestors' cumulative sweat, she shaped intricate patterns with her hands, as though weaving a piece of flamboyant cloth. Her dance was a conversation between her past and her present, an unspoken dialogue that elicited murmurs of appreciation from the audience.

Njegwe observed her, his eyes twinkling with pride, and stepped in. He had started to adopt Guatemalan symbols into his storytelling, contrasting stories of forest spirits and ancestral kings with the tales from Q'eqchi' or K'iche' tradition he had learned from the villagers. As his dark, sonorous voice filled the hushed crowd, he told stories of survival and promise.

As the music changed, the crowd grew comfortable and awaited the evening's main event, a collaboration of dance, song, and storytelling that was both an exchange of traditions and a rejection of separation.

Catalina began with a typical Guatemalan dance, her feet mimicking the pajá dance of the hummingbird, winged and frenetic and full of life. She moved amid stringed maracas and wooden flutes, forming a canopy above her, her body in shape and spirit evoking the quetzal, Guatemala's sacred bird, along with a symbol of freedom that flew with flamboyant feathers meant to deal destruction to warring tribes. Her eyes sparkled as she whirled, with such dexterity that the night air seemed to waver around her.

The villagers clapped along, some quietly singing the tune, others standing and watching in wonder. Catalina's voice and rhythm chimed with it as she called, "Vamos, corazón de la tierra!" which means "Come on, heart of the earth!" Her voice, rising in a joyful shout that felt as if it raised the whole square, too.

Then it was time for Njegwe's entrance, who moved to the resounding beat of *Madjon* and *Kana,* the Bamileke dances of community and strength. In his culture, the lion symbolized power, courage, and leadership, so his moves were inspired by the regal presence of the king of the jungle. In Western Cameroon kingdoms, the Lion is the totem of the kings. He imitated a lion's gait, a brave, strong, and protective stance. And then his hands balled into fists. They popped open wide, as though calling on the ancestors to bear witness to this moment of unity.

The spectators looked on in rapt attention as Njegwe's spinning became increasingly fluid, his power growing. "From our roots is strength; from our spirits, courage!" he roared in a voice that rolled like thunder across the empty space. The beat of his dance echoed through the words, igniting a fresh blaze of pride.

But together, the performers gelled without a seam across their traditions: Catalina's quick, fluttering movements meshed with Njegwe's low-to-the-ground power. It was like the dance had become a conversation, a visual story about two worlds coming together in harmony. Catalina's hands darted as if they were birds, while Njegwe's body glided with the commanding grace and the grunt of a lion pacing through the savannah. The populations were amazed to find that their differences melted into a common rhythm, proof of the power of diversity.

Soon, music slowed, and Njegwe and Catalina turned to one another, arms extended in a "handshake" of solidarity and respect. They had been conscious but measured, and they sealed a promise. They started communicating through expressive hand gestures. Catalina's hands flapped like a quetzal in flight, and Njegwe roared, pounding his fists gently against his chest.

The audience was on its feet at the sound of their steps, some whistling, more cheering as two figures danced in close formation, or danced away from each other and back toward one another again, their differences collapsing into common strength. It was a pure connection, an unspoken acknowledgment that their stories and spirits were forever intertwined.

As the celebration wound down, elders from both cultures came forward, offering small gifts: an embroidered huipil from a

Guatemalan grandmother, whose eyes were bright with pride; a carved wooden figure brought by a Cameroonian elder, its surface smoothed by years of devotion. The elders handed the symbols to Njegwe and Catalina, who received them with gratitude and respect.

Njegwe had a gentle way with him as he addressed the villagers and visitors: "Tonight we celebrate more than our traditions, including the magic that happens in uniting our traditions. Our spirits can fly and roar like the quetzal and the lion. Our stories, our dances, our songs are roots that reach deeper when we exchange and learn from each other."

Catalina then extended her trembling voice. "Our cultures are two rivers coming together, each with its own song and color. They become a new stream, full of life and possibility. When they meet, it becomes a new stream where we discover our strength."

The night went on with music and dancing, more shared feasts of corn tortillas and tamales, and roasted plantains spiced with pepper sauces. Children scampered through the square, threading their own tales with beads and feathers while their laughter mingled with the music. Elderly villagers passed on stories spanning generations, their voices thick with history and hope.

Under a sky filled with stars, Njegwe and Catalina perched on a bench, observing the spectacle before them. Njegwe looked at her and spoke softly: "You know, Catalina, it is in these moments when our worlds come together and make something new where we really learn about the power of roots and wings." He spoke quietly but with conviction.

Catalina looked at him, her eyes shining with tears of happiness. “Yes, Njegwe. We are making something sustainable here. A place where traditions can dance together, stories told without fear, and hope can fly.”

They remained still as they listened to voices and the distant sounds of music, feeling the community that was safe within them. Under those vigilant quetzal and lion eyes, hope flew higher than ever before, a lasting reminder that even in exile, roots and wings could grow together into a skyward future where unity, respect, and dreams were shared.

Chapter 15: The Crown of the Exile

It was an easy, early dawn in the village, and the sky streamed a soft, golden light that seemed to breathe new life into the earth. There was an expectation in the air, a stillness that portended change. Today was no ordinary day. It was a day of rebirth, when Njegwe assumed his new name, one that didn't include exile but rather resilience and purpose, and a limping sense of collective hope.

The people had formed a circle at the center, where the light was strongest, their faces gleaming with awe and expectation. The rays of early morning sunlight filtered through the leaves, creating mottled patterns on their skin. In the center of the circle was Njegwe, not in refugee or outsider's clothing, but clad in a cape sewn from the stories, symbols, and traditions of his birthplace and his new home. There was a story in every stitch, every thread, telling of adversity met, roots penetrating deep, and futures forged.

His head was not encircled with gold or jewels, but with a band of twisted creepers, dotted with blossoms, and adorned on one side with an ornament that glittered as though it bloomed by night and faded with the morning light. The crown sparkled in the morning sun as a living picture of growth, resilience, and the sacred link to nature and ancestors. It was a crown of humility and hope, not one of power.

Catalina came out from behind him, holding a minuscule carved stick, that small, cherished talisman from her childhood forests, handed down by her grandmother. The staff was carved from a single piece of wood and engraved with symbols of animals, spirits, and plants, each guardian over her family's stories and traditions. With her walked priests and elders from the village bearing offerings: a woven fabric embroidered with Cameroonian designs, a bowl of holy herbs perfumed with jasmine and sage, and a quetzal feather plucked at dawn from trees that kept silent vigil over them.

Njegwe felt his heart racing as the ceremony began. The old man from the village stepped forward, his voice calm and respectful but thick with emotion.

"Today, we celebrate your journey not as an exile but as one planted seed, a reborn spirit," he said, his eyes twinkling with pride. "You have stood your history with grace, and now you stand here as a symbol of hope for all of us."

He gently clasped Njegwe's hand and, with almost sacred care, set the circlet on his head. The old one's voice, heavy and evenly measured, chanted the inherited words from generations past, words of rebirth, strength, and solidarity. "May this crown be a reminder to you that you are no longer just a survivor, but a keeper of stories, jester of the courts, and bearer of dreams. May it serve as a reminder that you have roots and they, too, run deep, and that your branches are always toward heaven."

Njegwe shut his eyes as the crown was placed upon him. Tactalate, a traditional drink made of roasted cacao with ground rice and pine nuts, was pressed lightly against his forehead and pieces of Mexico around him. It was light, but it was not weak, and it carried a symbol not of power, but of responsibility. An acceptance that he was the protector of a new community, a bridge between cultures, a living testament to resilience reborn.

He snatched it from Catalina's hands and held it up. Holding it high, he looked at the assembled villagers, men, women, and children, each face filled with anticipation. Their combined breath seemed to catch, as if they were all bound together in this holy moment.

"I am not simply Njegwe the exile," he said in a voice that was clear and strong, carrying through their silence. "Today, I am transformed into Njegwe, the protector of roots, stories, and future generations. I have the strength of my foremothers, and I honor the bravery of this place. We rise together, we grow together, and we create a new path, one that is based on love, respect, and shared purpose".

The people in the village burst into applause, some with tears glistening in their eyes, others smiling with quiet pride. Children were shouting and clapping their hands as if there had never been any doubt, their innocence reflecting the hope that filled the air, though that hope was rebounding. Elders nodded in somber agreement; their faces etched with the weight of years. All around the forest seemed silent, hushed in reverence of this moment, nature its own witness.

But even as they rejoiced, word of Njegwe's work and leadership soon spread far beyond their village. Whispers were carried across the winds by traders and travelers who frequented the adjacent communities. Before long, envoys and elders came from afar with gifts and tales of their own hardships and aspirations. They arrived with offerings of grains, weavings, and carved symbols that represented their mutual desire for peace and unity.

And then, into a redolent gathering of sacred herbs and filled with the sound of drums echoing through the trees, came local kings and chieftains. A few were on horseback, their steel gleaming in the sun; others made a calm, respectful entrance, walking down to the center with eyes filled with wonder. Their appearance transformed the moment into a glorious celebration of the people's power.

And with rapt attention, they heard Njegwe recount his journey as a stranger who had become a healer of wounds and a weaver of bridges. What he said struck home and moved the people deeply.

Swayed by his tail, the kings and council members began speaking to one another in excited voices, filled with wonder and possibility. They spoke of an ancient tradition whispered about in their legends: that it was not enough to be born to the throne, but that one must serve and free others through action. With new eyes, they began to look at Njegwe; there was one who embodied their ancestral virtues: a great heart, a wise mind, and a strong arm.

The old man from Njegwe's village came forward again and spoke with authority. "Your work has planted seeds of unity and hope beyond our borders. The people here look at you and see the power of their ancestors. If you are willing, the land wishes to honor you as more than their protector, but as their king."

Silence seemed to descend upon the gathering. Niegwe glanced from face to face, the villagers, elders, kings, and beyond them to the mountains, his eyes distant with unseeing eyes as though he were barely present at that moment. His heart danced with humble gratitude.

He drew in a sharp breath, then shook his head lightly with a small, genuine smile. "I am humbled," he said, "but my crown is not made of gold. It is made of the stories we tell, the roots we plant, and the hope that we carry. It is the will of the people that I am now called upon to serve. I have never aspired to power but have always fought against it, and that naturally emboldens me to accept this honor more than if it had been given to me by one of those rare concurrences by which a man is chosen without seeking office. And I promise to serve with humility, strength, and most of all, love."

The kings and the elders nodded in assent to the cheers of the crowd, who began dancing, singing, and clapping in jubilation. That day represented not only Njegwe's rebirth but also the birth of a new world, one in which exile and roots, tradition and innovation were woven together into a fabric of collective sovereignty.

And as the sun rose higher, enveloping the land in a gentle golden light, he looked out at the community he had adopted as his new home. His path from exile to leader, from outsider to king, was woven into the fabric of the land, a testament to the truth that even when we are separated, true sovereignty grows from common heritage and shared destiny.

Chapter 16: Embracing the Inner Land

Night's velvet curtain had descended over the land, deep and silent. Njegwe stood on the outskirts of the village, clustered beneath an old tree with branches that spread like a great umbrella and roots that dug into the earth. Its leaves rustled secrets to the wind softly. The moon hung luminously and full, bathing the landscape in silver light.

He sat with his back against the damp, cool grass and gazed past the darkness, out where he knew a faint path to his homeland awaited. The night was very still, but a tempest of conflicting emotions raged within him: fear and excitement, grief and hope, doubt and steel-willed determination. Every breath he took seemed weighed up with the significance of this moment: years of exile, years of his ancestors' longings, generations of hopes from his children, and all the dreams he had for himself.

"Am I truly ready"? He became obsessed, hearing the question carved in the empty cavities of his brain. It wasn't just a crossing of borders; the journey was an exploration of himself, questioning his identity, purpose, and essence. Having carried the weight of separation and desire for so many years, simply thinking of going back to his homeland filled him with both quivering longings and terrifying tremors.

He reached out to touch the carved talisman that hung between his breasts and over his heart, a gift from Catalina, a piece of unassuming wood etched with sacred figures: animals, spirits, and plants woven into ancestral amulets. The smooth surface jolted his fingers, coolness cutting through the chaos. And in the silence of the night, he recited a long prayer, asking for guidance from his ancestors, the land, and, most importantly, himself.

Guide me. Strengthen me. May this return be more than a crossing of land, may it be a crossing into truth, into healing, into purpose. His voice was little more than a breath, dredged gently into the night. The spirits did not answer with words, but he felt their presence in the rustling of leaves around him and in the thud-thud music of his blood.

It's more than a physical return, he mused. It is also a spiritual rebirth, shucking off the shame of exile and reclaiming roots long buried under the pain of separation. He thought of his ancestors, their stories written in the sand and fleshed out by generations lost to history, cursed and blessed with love, war, and time. Their voices rang faint yet insistent, urging him forward.

Their hopes live in my blood. He thought. I am both exiled and homecoming, survivor and healer. This journey is about crossing borders, those dictated by circumstance, by history, by fear. It is about getting myself into what I am supposed to become. He could feel the weight of his ancestors' spirits leaning gently against him, directing him and reminding him that he was part of a legacy that could not be broken.

Tonight, I am no longer a man who comes out from exile, but a vessel of hope, and the bridge between worlds. His desire crystallized as he called out into the darkness: "I am coming back not to conquer you, but to visit you." Not to seize power, but to introduce myself to you". The strength of my ancestors runs through me, their stories my armor.

The night was heavy with significance, every star a witness to his inarticulate pledges. It was a big dream, but the world lay before him, waiting to be lived, inspiring tales of rebirth and resilience. He saw among the pulsing stars the faces of his ancestors, guiding him, watching over him, beckoning him toward his fate.

Then, in solitude in their humble home, Njegwe sat next to Catalina, their children playing around, small palms cradling artifacts of their collective past: braided bracelets, embroidered linen, chiseled figures. Suddenly, the air was thick with quiet softness, a holy ground where hearts and dreams met.

Njegwe looked into Catalina's eyes and saw her fierce pride and her quiet strength. And with that look, the shared knowledge that while he was undertaking this journey alone, it was one they were all on together. The kids looked up, wide-eyed and innocent, clenching the trinkets of their heritage, reminders of their origins and struggles.

He caressed the tops of their heads in the gentlest way and spoke with a soft voice, "Tomorrow we will travel to where I was born, our land, your home, and walk knowing that every step we take is along a path laid by those who came before us." There was an emotion in his voice then, a vow made of hope and determination.

The children nodded, solemn but innocent trust filling their faces. Catalina's hand tightened around him. In that moment, they all realized this is not a mere physical travel, it is an inner spirit journey, a bringing back of identity, a revival of hope.

As the morning hours drew closer, Njegwe deliberately relaxed in their modest space. He looked at the carved stuff and then glanced at the symbols etched into its surface; glyphs, guardians of their legacy, each symbolizing ancestors who lived before them, stories shared in dark night gatherings, hopes expressed by whispering winds. He made a small pack: a bit of the earth from their land, some token from Catalina's forests, something to keep from his childhood.

Stepping out into the waking world, his eyes set on her, a small boat bobbing at the edge of a slip, roughened but seaworthy, wood tell-tale tokens of dented life faithfully. His heart raced, a blend of appreciation and determination. Each motion was intentional: the packing, the final glance at his family, the wordless prayer.

He drew a breath and filled his lungs with cool morning air. Balancing carefully, his hands crossed over the window of the car, driving to the airport. Each kilometer crossed brings them closer to the land where he was born. He left the country alone, and now, he is coming back with a wife from a foreign country and mixed children. The travel itself was a sacred act that represented crossing boundaries: mental, emotional, and cultural.

The car rides slowly, pushing forward through a well-maintained lane of asphalt, traveling to a land that had once been his and now awaited him, calling him home. It was a crossing of many territorial and spatial borders, geographical, spiritual, and cultural, with every paddle a prayer of hope.

When Njegwe understood the crew was announcing the remaining flying time to his motherland, his heartbeat quickened. Through the window, he can see rolling hills, the sway of ancient trees, the whisper of wind, surely not just landscapes but living memories waiting to wrap themselves around him.

When they landed at Douala International Airport, Njegwe kissed the tarmac and began a monologue: Here I am, Cameroon.

I left you, and I am back not to take power but to pay you tribute, to respect you, to honor you. I left alone, but I am coming back with your wife, your children. Accept them, please". Earth embraced him not like a stranger but as a son, still welcome after a long loss. It was not only a homecoming in the physical sense, but it was also a spiritual renaissance, a reclaiming of self and identity.

After the checkout process, they embraced the Feu (King), the Queen, the notable, the siblings, and other affiliated royal staff, and embarked on the journey to West Cameroon. Now the sun was rising on this land, and golden warmth covered it with a shining promise. Njegwe looked to the horizon, his ancestors' spirits speaking on the breeze. The second half of his life started today, and one can only hope that it will be a chapter ushering in unity, healing, and hope.

Chapter 17: Two Kingdoms, One Heart

The sun was high and golden in the sky, casting blessings over a lush land where two worlds, Cameroon and Guatemala, had finally begun to connect, their shared history and desires forming a point of unity so profound. Seas had parted them, and mountains had barred the way, but now distance melted before a common conscience and a shared heart that beat louder with every pulse in the public space of the newly reinforced village, a tapestry of cultures unfurled with pride. Seated in the woven chairs were wise old men with lines etched into their faces, holding staffs of wood so sacred that any maggot within a mile would die if it drank from them. Their loose garments were rimmed in symbols embroidered by past generations. Chiefs and leaders from both groups gathered, each bringing symbols of their culture: vibrantly colored textiles embroidered with elaborate patterns, carved wooden objects adorned with feathers or animals, and jewelry glistening with glass beads and gemstones, every piece a token of endurance and a marker of identity.

Today was a celebration of the bond that adversity forged, hope, and the untiring human spirit that could not be conquered by distance or history. It was a day to celebrate the ties that had formed through shared struggles and dreams.

At the head stood Njegwe, now crowned and recognized as a king, the living symbol of a bridge between two worlds, two dimensions. His posture was firm, his face calm yet radiant with belief. His family flanked him: Catalina, glowing with pride, and the children, wide-eyed and inquisitive, each clutching a trinket from their past.

His voice was clear and resolute, yet humble and hopeful. “We declare today,” he began “that the alliance of our communities is more than an alliance; It is a union. We proclaim our strength in our differences. These two lands, Cameroon and Guatemala, may be far apart, but they are now bound by purpose: to forge a future of mutual respect, share wisdom, and lasting friendship. Our differences are our foundation, and as one, they create a mosaic far more beautiful than any single piece could achieve on its own.”

Then the elder of the Cameroonian village handed over a carved emblem of strength and freedom, an image of a lion and a quetzal interlocked on a wooden disk. His voice was deep and steady, shaped by years of tradition. “Our ancestors understood,” he said, “that true power does not come at the expense of another’s strength but rather from knowing one’s own place in the world. The real power emerges when cultures join hands and reach out to one another, when kings stand with commoners and warriors with healers. Today, I want us to commit to ensuring that the next generation remains politically, culturally, and spiritually linked, so that our children inherit from us a future in unity and respect.”

A respected community leader from Guatemala, her face full of warmth and kindness, stepped forward. Her voice was clear and sincere. “Our stories vary, but our dreams are universal,” she said. “We want peace, prosperity, and dignity for all our children. We understand that, in collaboration, through sharing our traditions, our wisdom, and our leadership, we can build a better tomorrow than any one of us could ever dream. For our hopes are shared, and together they guide us forward.”

The ceremony, filled with music, dance, and symbolic gift exchanges. Representatives from both communities approached with offerings: textile banners woven with symbols from both cultures, bowls of traditional foods such as spiced soups and sweet plantains, and sacred objects carved or embroidered with ancestral motifs. Every gift was a symbol of respect, a connection between their stories and their hopes. They came to an agreement: an alliance of hearts and minds that cemented their communities in complicity, mutual endeavor, and a shared fate.

The Njegwe family was awarded titles reflecting their role as emissaries of unity. Catalina was gifted with a necklace of feathers and beads symbolizing the flight of the Quetzal and her spirit. Their children, dressed in crossbred Cameroonian and Guatemalan clothing, bright textiles, and embroidered patterns punctuated with beads, were offered tiny tokens: woven bracelets, embroidered clothing, a reminder of their common history, and a hope for future generations.

As the celebration unfolded, stories of their ancestors' histories unfolded, tales crossing borders, fighting for justice, and celebrating life in song and dance. Elders from both tribes exchanged lessons in kinship, respect, and the continuing importance of maintaining ties to culture even as new ties were forged. The air was rich with the perfume of roasted plantains, spiced meat, and pungent herbs, mingled with drumbeats, marimba tunes, and, yes, the voices of storytellers bringing history vividly to life, to flesh-and-blood memory.

Later, as the sun lowered near the horizon, Njegwe rose once more and raised his hands to silence the crowd. His speech was calm, but he commanded the stage. "Two kingdoms, two cultures, but one heart," he proclaimed. "Now we are embraced by a history that is shared and rich, wider than any ocean, and deeper than any inheritance. Patrimony, and as citizens of this earth, we are a part of a family that not only struggles together but also smiles together. We should celebrate our differences and what brings us together: our human spirit. In diversity, there is richness; in unity, there is strength."

The audience cheered, clapped, and sang. Around them, children ran and played, their laughter carried by the wind, while old men exchanged knowing glances, caught my eye, and nodded slightly with quiet satisfaction, their smiles quiet.

The night air turned slightly chill, and lanterns were lit, casting a warm shimmer over the scene. The fire popped, sparks exploding into the evening sky, signaling a community's welcome to this new chapter, based not on repression but on respect, love, and mutual commitment.

Since that day, councils and committees have been formed under common auspices to work together on planning exchanges, schools, and joint assistance projects. Schools in both villages began teaching each other's languages and stories, intertwining their histories into a common fabric. Festivals blended elements of both cultures, including dances of lions and quetzals, drumming and marimba, and textile weaving and/or wood carving, all interwoven as an expression of unity within difference.

Neighbors helped neighbors, elders shared stories of perseverance, and leaders uplifted one another's visions for a better future. It cemented the Cameroonian Guatemalan relationship as living proof that when there is understanding, respect, and shared dreams, nothing meaningful is impossible.

Yet in every heart, young or old, there remains one simple truth: when two worlds meet with respect and love, they somehow find a way to become one. Two kingdoms, one heart, a shielded legacy of resilience and hope. That's the indomitable human spirit shining across the nation.

Chapter 18: The Wedding Under the Ceiba Tree

The sun warmed the countryside of Guatemala, where everything was so green and beautiful. A golden afternoon light washed over the village, softening all the leaves and stones until they seemed almost alive. The atmosphere was rife with energy and bliss as the scents and sounds of blooming flowers, roasted corn, and fragrant herbs filled the air. In the center of this sacred gathering stood the formidable Ceiba tree, a towering symbol of life, unity, and ancestral connection, with its wide-branching arms whispering stories in the gusts of wind above.

Today's ceremony was a wedding like no other. It was a religious reaffirmation of love, a bridge between two worlds. It felt like a personal reunion of families once separated by oceans, mountains, and hardship. It was a scene of cultural pride, ancestral blessing, and familial communion. "There is a profound way so much sense, when you pass through a ceremony like this, that it carries the weight of generations of realized hopes, realities fulfilled, and honored histories," Njegwe said.

Percussion from a distance and the sweet, high-pitched hum of marimbas blended in harmony, weaving the rhythms of Cameroon with those of Guatemala. Women in brilliant huipils, their embroidered textiles glistening in the sun, gathered in circles with bright faces lit by joy and reverence. Men in woven shirts, heavily decorated with fine beadwork, danced elegantly, their movement echoing ancestral dances. Repeatedly, blessing words were spoken in simple, whispered words that were deeply felt. Elders from both cultures sat together, side by side, eyes shining with hope and pride.

The honored and special guest was Njegwe's father, the Feu (King). He wore an extravagant feathered headdress, beaded necklaces dangling over multicolored embroidered robes stitched with symbols of royal lineage that referenced superior kingship, and he walked or strode with the sensual majesty of a man who had been trained for generations to reign. His bearing was such that his presence alone inspired respect, and Njegwe saw that he was deeply moved, his eyes shining with a little pride and much emotion as he walked towards his son.

Njegwe's father stopped at the edge of the group's gathering and raised his hand in blessing. The crowd hushed in anticipation. And then, in a deep, resonant voice, trumpet-like, he spoke to the gathering around him. "And today we celebrate not only the marriage of two souls," he declared, "but also the convergence of two legacies Cameroon and Guatemala joined in love and respect, sharing a common destiny."

He stepped up beside Njegwe, who appeared small under the spreading tree's overarching limbs. The village's elders raised a carved wooden emblem, a representation of kingship and guardianship, etched with intertwined images of lions and quetzal, symbolizing strength and freedom. He raised it high and offered it to Njegwe and then spoke with great respect. "They knew," he continued, his voice steady, "that true power comes not from harming others but from bringing them together, of turning them into allies, even friends. That is cultivated when we lift one another up." Today, we commit to lifting and honoring their love, spiritually, culturally, and politically for the health of all our children and generations to come."

Catalina moved forward, her bright huipil embroidered with animals, flowers, and celestial symbols in the colors of her homeland. In her hands, she held a bouquet laced with wild herbs, feathers, and minuscule charms, each symbolizing hope, perseverance, and her sacred ties to the natural world. Her emotionally charged voice cut softly above the gentle hum of merriment. "Love," she whispered, "is the most powerful thread we all possess. It transcends borders, oceans, and adversity. Today, I honor not just Njegwe, but the beating of our hearts together and the hope of a future in which our cultures may thrive side by side, entwined in harmony."

She saw Njegwe, dressed in his traditional Cameroonian attire, a dress of an embroidered tunic, beaded necklaces, and a cloth wrapped around his waist, delicately holding her hands. His gaze was steady and dark as if it met hers. "From the jungles of Cameroon to the hills of Guatemala," he said, his voice filled with certainty, "our love has taught us that understanding, friendship, and patience are the universal counterparts to kinship. Hatred and division are mirages, and the shadows they cast grow larger when we peel our eyes from one another to gaze into the void of all that we wish to avoid. And today, we remind each other that the most transcendent principle of love is that it is a powerful force that no barrier can hinder it."

The Feu, dignified, deep-voiced, and radiant in golden and colorful regalia, spoke again. He raised his hand, a staff carved with images of his ancestors' lions, quetzals, and sacred designs, interwoven in a dance of lineage. "My son," he spoke with pride thick in his voice, "your quest has taught us that true kingship is based on love, humility, and tenacity. "My generation brought you what we inherited, and now, I hand over the blessings of our ancestors to you and bestow upon you the honor of carrying our shared heritage into a bright future."

And so, he carefully passed the royal staff to Njegwe, and its carvings glistened in the sun. "Let this staff declare your calling, not merely as a leader but as a protector of kin and a nurturer of our collective dreams. You are now a living representation of strength, unity, and hope."

Family members and elders of Dje surrounded them, raising their voices in song and prayer, ancient blessings that defied language yet filled the sacred space.

At the service's climactic moment, the community burst into dance, drummers pounding ecstatic rhythms and dancers threading through the gathering throng in a joyous celebration of life and kinship. Cameroonian and Guatemalan traditional dances intertwined lions and quetzals, marimbas and drums, each footfall a declaration of resilience and love. The air hummed with joy, respect, and the joined heartbeat of two cultures settling as one.

A grand feast followed under the wide, great spreading branches of Ceiba, with laden tables from both lands: spicy stews, tamales, roasted yams, and plantains. There was a story in every bite, a memory attached to each flavor. Children imitated the dances they had witnessed, their laughter rising like a chorus of hope, an affirmation of life and tradition.

In an intimate, soulful moment, Njegwe and Catalina shared rings, clear, simple symbols of their vows. As they interlace their fingers, smiling to one another and whispering promises, they showed that love's greatest strength lies in understanding one another deeply in compassion for another's suffering, as Christ showed through His own sacrifice, and in sharing the same dreams. Their marriage was a living testimony that love based on respect and friendship can form indestructible bridges across oceans and continents.

The Feu of Dje stepped forward once again as twilight let the stars dance, and lanterns played to a gentle night breeze. He made some remarks in his native language with solemnity; his tone was grave and melodious. "May this union be a light," he said, "a reminder that love, respect, and understanding are the highest kingdoms of life. We can only build a future worthy of our ancestors' dreams if we stand together as one people, in kinship, hope, and peace."

Under the mighty Ceiba, enveloped by family and friends, and spirits of both the living and the ancestral nature, it was a wedding far greater than a simple celebration of love. It was a testimony to the lasting force of kinship across borders, through hardships, and overtime. It was a living, breathing reminder that we all speak the language of the heart, a universal language that united us in hope, perseverance, and undying love. And under the sacred branches of Ceiba, Njegwe and Catalina's love was reborn, deeper, stronger, and more rooted than ever, carrying the teachings of resilience, togetherness, and shared destiny forward for generations to come.

Chapter 19: Roots and Reveries

As the final rays of sunset turned to twilight, Njegwe quietly slipped away from the happy gathering beneath the Ceiba's towering branches. The rhythm of the music lingered in memory through his closed eyelids, but there inside himself, another melody summoned, a whisper from long ago when his roots first reached down into sacred soil from which he had grown as a child.

He steadied himself, shaking from the shrine's field, pressing his hands against the soft moss that covered the shrine's grassy floor. Kneeling on the cold ground, he closed his eyes. The present dissolved, falling away in an instant, and he was back in the forests of Cameroon, where the sacred groves stretched endlessly and ancient limbs reached toward the sky like the arms of ancestral spirits searching for connection. He recalled climbing mango, kola, and plum trees for the first time. Those watchful sentinels of the land that bore stories within their bark, stories of kings and spirits, of ancestors who had danced and murmured beneath them. Each step forward was a step into a world where the spirits were alive, and every leaf was a page in an open book of history, waiting there for him to listen.

The air was heavy with the smell of wet soil, crushed leaves, and yams roasting over fires at twilight. His tiny hands clung to the dry, coarse bark, fingers tracing its ridges as though reading sacred inscriptions. The trees, he believed, were not just living things but also keepers of memory and guardians of stories passed down through generations.

He remembered it as he walked under the biggest tree, gaze lost in the intricate network of shadows and sunlight woven above him, a filigree. His grandmother's lulling voice would soar into repetitive song as she recounted tales of their forebears, the fabulous kings and brave warriors, till-roving spirits that danced in the leaves. "Shhhh," she'd whisper, "the forest sings if you listen with your heart. It is the voice of those who have gone before, calling out your name in the breeze."

It was the dances, those dances before a village's glow and fire, the sacred rituals under a lazy moon in its full strength. The casting of bitter kola across his mouth and that fresh feeling when cool water draped itself across his skin. These memories were more than images; they were living strands woven into his soul, binding him to the land and its spirits.

Then he was swiftly brought back to reality by a soft voice, Catalina, as though her words were wafted through the mist of some far-away dream and settled lightly upon his mind. She was talking about the sacred ceiba tree in her village, its giant trunk serving as a ladder between worlds, its roots extending into the underworld, and its branches stretching toward the heavens.

"In my village," she whispered, "le ceiba is more than a tree. That's the pulse of the universe. It is where the spirits of our ancestor's rest, where prayers rise like smoke, and from which new dreams are born. When I sit in its boughs, I feel them guiding me, forgiving me, reminding me who I am."

Njegwe opened his eyes and met hers with the same reverence that had always filled him under Cameroon's sacred forests. The stories, the ghosts, the signs crossed borders, joining two worlds in the root and sky's sacred tongue.

He took her hand, holding it lightly and feeling in the warmth, in the strength, and in the heartbeat of common kinship. "Maybe our roots," he said softly, "come from different soils, but they grow in the same sacred ground, here, right now, and in this world-spanning love."

He remembered so many nights wandering through the forest, listening to spirit talk, feeling Earth as a living thing beneath his feet. Those memories were like sacred beads, threaded lesson by lesson with resilience, patience, and humility. They had taught him that roots are delicate but not fragile, and that they tether us when storms come and buoy us toward hope when despair sets in.

But Catalina's gentle yet firm voice brought him back to the here and now. She was telling the stories she had heard about the spiritual significance of the ceiba, how her ancestors considered it the axis of the universe, linking the underworld to earth and the heavens. "When I'm sitting under it," she said, "I can feel the spirits of my ancestors whispering in its leaves and reminding me that I am never alone. My journey is just part of a larger story."

Njegwe heard in her voice a deep kinship and knew that their histories may have come from different lands, but they were lines drawn through the same holy cloth of life, spirit, and memory. The voices of their forebears, silent but powerful, resonated in their collective respect for Mother Nature.

He gave her hand, which he still held in a soft squeeze. Somehow, the bonds between them had deepened with each other's unspoken understanding. "Our roots," he said, quietly, "are not just in the earth, but also woven into stories and spirits that guide us. We have them in our blood, inside of a dream, and with each breath."

As Njegwe watched the first stars twinkle into life, he knew that this was no mere memory or myth passed down from ancestor to descendant; it was a living manifestation of their common fate. They would grow and spread their roots, strong from the soil of their forebears, in love with new futures watered with respect, knowledge, and hope.

Underneath the mighty Ceiba, encircled by spirits of the earth and sky, Njegwe was filled with one undeniable truth: to respect one's past is to carry its stories forward so that love and memory remain alive through generations. The sacred trees, the tales in their shade, and the spirits that whispered with the wind were the gifts that carried them past exile and into a future where roots knew flight, bonded forever by something indestructible and eternal.

Chapter 20: Echoes of the Ancestors

As they quietly returned after the rejoicing in the shadow of the giant Ceiba, Njegwe and Catalina felt an invisible hand drawing them to a more sacred, open space at the center of their village, where whispers of ancient ceremonies still hung in the air. The sky had draped itself in dark indigo, the stars poking through to pierce the darkness, causing faint crackles of light that flickered and danced like ghosts circling each other around their own fire.

This was a sanctuary where earth remembered, where their mentors came as unseen, invited witnesses to the union, protectors of her origins, and bearers of hope. It was a hallowed space, molded by time and tradition, where memory and spirit coiled together like the taproots of sacred trees that had witnessed so many rites of passage.

Njegwe's thoughts returned to the hidden groves of Cameroon, secret spots shrouded in morning mists where elders once performed rites to call on the spirits of the land. The thumping of drums, the crash and burn of crushed herbs and roosters sanctified by fire, low chanting murmured prayers, ... these were the sounds that had stitched through his childhood like a sacred tapestry of belonging and awe. The ritual practices had been a language that predated words, one told with symbols carved into wood, stone, and earth itself.

Her name was Catalina, and her voice was so gentle and powerful. She began to recount stories of her ancestors, the Nahuatl tales of offerings in sacred mountains, and the cacao ritual, a moment when they gave everything to thank and be reborn. She thought of her elders who gathered at dawn, each offering tobacco, flowers, and something small that belonged to them, a prayer to the spirits of earth and sky.

It was the patchwork we shared, woven from the memories of those who came before us. Her words reverberated with the rhythm of her ancestors' chants, beating in sync with the heart of her lineage.

The first two advanced into the ring of the elders, and the firelight played upon their faces as they stood. As if on cue, the old men, whose eyes were as deep as the ocean and as steady as ancient mountains, began a slow, deliberate chant that rose and fell like wind through sacred forests.

Njegwe, solemn, looked on as a young woman with respectful hands drew from a woven basket the sacred herbs she poured into the flame: bay leaves, sage, sweet-smelling cinnamon, and cedar crushed to bits. As the herbs encountered the fire, a sweet-smelling smoke rose into the sky, curling and burning like a prayer into the invisible world. The scent was earthy, energizing, and replete with memories of sacred forests and ancestors' blessings.

Catalina advanced, holding a carved feather from the sacred quetzal in her hand, the iridescent colors catching the firelight. She set it down gently on the altar, a murmured invocation of thanks to the spirits of her fathers, those who had lived through persecution, whose strength she carried in her flesh and bones. Hers was a lullaby, a tender span of closeness between her body and the divine.

The elders circulated tokens, small carved images, and symbols that represented their bloodlines: a wooden lion from Njegwe's Cameroon, the animal an emblem of strength and royalty, a silken quetzal feather from Catalina's Guatemala, an icon of freedom and transcendence, a handful of rich earth from each respective land, teeming with the lifeblood of their ancestors' soil. Every object was a holy seedling, suggesting that roots went deeper than ground cover, to memory, faith, and sacred obligation.

In the drum's relentless thumping, which resounded within him, he felt the accompaniment of those who had gone before, echoes of his childhood, his homeland, and his spirits. He inhaled the aroma of the charred herbs and felt his ancestors' pulse in his veins like a sanctified current.

The older of the two elders dipped fingers into a small gourd half-filled with water. He sowed droplets over the fire, over the tokens, over the congregation that had gathered, and each droplet was a benediction and a supplication for succor, each a prayer for regeneration. The water bubbled gently as it hit the flames and became vapor, ascending like prayers into the night.

His heartbeat expanded as the whispers of his ancestors greeted him in the wind, hummed in the rustling leaves, murmured through cracks and embers, and echoed in an abyss somewhere deep inside. Those were echoes of resilience, from people who had stood firm and lived through events so powerful and intense that their stories reverberated beneath my feet.

He put his own token, a small carved lion from Cameroon, on the altar with trembling hands. He held it as a symbol of kingship, bravery, and protection. It was a reminder that the belonging of his bloodline had its roots in something much deeper than borders, beyond even the dimensions of space and time, deep within those known-only-to-God heartbeats of his unbroken lineage of persecuted, displaced, exiled forebears.

Njegwe closed his eyes once more, hearing the soft, pulsating drumbeat and feeling the sacred force moving within him. He saw the ghosts of his land, the forest guardians, and ancestral kings, and sacred grove-spirits, gathered in a vast circle, rejoicing in his passage, blessing his marriage to Catalina as they redoubled their secret vow to protect him.

And in that sacred instant, he knew that those rituals, the conjuring of spirits, the offerings, the chants themselves were a necessity. They were the pulsing blood of his being, the spiritual seeds that linked him to the history and future of his people. “These were the echoes of his ancestors, the unseen roots holding him up, giving him strength and resilience that allowed hope to take root”.

The voices fell to a low whisper as the chant dwindled away, and Njegwe and Catalina clasped hands and simply said, "Thanks." The flickering firelight cast a glow on their faces, and it was clear they were united in a vow that their love had been found not so much in the here and now in the sacred blood of ancient ancestors.

And in the darkening of the village, it was as if even the spirits of the land exhaled a blessing on them, and ancient, holy benediction carried through the breath of trees, a riddle that travels across eons: "Your roots are forever. Your spirits are alive. Your story unfolds as that of those who came before”.

Chapter 21: Roots in Exile

A flood of golden amber sunlight showered the land, casting long, slender shadows across lush scenery. Under the sheltering boughs of the powerful Ceiba tree, guardian of life, ancestors, and dreams, Njegwe rested in silent meditation. Stories of triumph and renewal took root under its earthbound reach, gleaning hope and the sweep of its canopy, whispering in the indescribable, ancient secrets. The leaves shivered, rustling against one another like the murmur of ancestors resonating across decades, whispering stories of hardship and love that knew no boundaries, hardship that birthed strength.

His family members huddled closely around him, their faces peaceful and glowing in the dimming light. They said it all with the weight and wonder of the journey they had made together across their brows, eyes that held the wounds of exile as well as those that glistened with new beginnings. Catalina was seated at his side, her hand resting lightly on his shoulder and a calm, proud glint in her eye. Their young children, sweet and innocent, sat cross-legged on the soft grass before them, tiny fists clutching souvenirs from exotic places: feathers from Guatemala, beads from Cameroon, tiny woven charms that linked their worlds.

Exile had entwined their years into a great, living tapestry, every thread a fiber of love and tenderness, resistance and hope. And even though borders and seas separated them, they never felt more than a breadth apart, anchored by countless visits, shared stories, and exchanged traditions. The children's trips to Cameroon were sacred pilgrimages, moments of reclamation where they reclaimed their language, danced their ancestors' dances, and sat at the feet of elders to soak up stories that had traveled through generations. These journeys deepened their knowledge and understanding that belonging was not restricted to one soil but lay in the heart's ability to foster new attachments wherever they might take root.

Njegwe looked at his family and bit back the tenderness, letting his thoughts drift to the lessons exile had hewn into him, lessons scratched across his soul like sacred images. Exile had taught him that roots were fragile and could easily break but could also grow strong and resilient through hardship. The hardships, the losses, were seeds implanted in his spirit, and they had grown into iron-like resilience.

The letter he had received recently was from the newly elected officials of the country that had deported Njegwe. It offered official recognition of their unjust deportation. The letter expressed regret and invited him to visit to share his story in a broader context, and participate in discussions about his experience, but Njegwe, with quiet dignity and humility, had refused.

He traced the surface of the earth under the tree with his fingers, sensing its cool, damp solidity. "That unfortunate deportation," he whispered softly, "is what led me to my true destiny. It was a harrowing chapter of anger, confusion, and loss, but also one that forced me to realize that my roots are not tied to any one land or moment in time. My travels have taught me that resiliency and love are the most important inheritance we can pass on."

He looked at his wonder-filled, bright-eyed, still-kid-curious children and whispered to Catalina. "Our roots are grounded in resilience and love. They may be planted in remote lands, but the fruits they bear share common humanity wherever we tend them, whether through our actions, our stories, or the connections we forge for future generations". His voice was low but assured.

The leaves rustled gently in the wind, as though they were whispering a lullaby, forever repeating the story of planting, growing, ending what has ended, and beginning again, always ending what has passed and always beginning anew. The family remained in reflective silence, attuned to the melody of nature's music and feeling the unspoken promise that their journey was a continuum of nurturing roots and sowing hope in the rich soil of love and understanding.

It occurred to Njegwe that we must have shared a thousand holidays, celebrations, and exchanged stories between families, each testament that exile had been the end but merely a chapter in a greater story of transformation. The children's trips to Cameroon, during which they embraced their cultural roots, reaffirmed that belonging was an organic, ever-evolving thing rooted in the heart's capacity to love across backgrounds.

He conjured images of loved ones, elders sharing lessons on resilience, children dancing in the sunlight, young men and women forging new paths, and he felt grateful and responsible. Under Ceiba, Njegwe silently pledged to keep nourishing these roots, to honor the ancestors who had suffered so much, and to transmit the lessons of perseverance, love, and unity to generations yet unborn.

He knew that belonging was not just about place, but a complex weave of stories, attachments, and spirits. It lived in all the acts of kindness, every story passed on, and in gestures of love unfettered by frontiers. It resided in the souls of those who learned to love without inhibition, to take root in hope, however far or hard the soil.

And so, in the silent strength forged by exile and transformed into a foundation of power, Njegwe's legacy finally took hold more deeply than it ever could have before. It was entwined with the dreams of his children, the love of his family, and the lasting bonds that crossed oceans and continents. His roots were deep, strong, and unassailable, his feet planted in a future grounded in hope, unity, and determination.

Roots in exile. Roots in love. Roots that stretch into the future, thick and eternal, always connected.

Under the watchful limbs of ancient Ceiba, Njegwe felt it in his heart: that home is not a place but a way of being, a story we carry, and an enduring love that knows no borders. And in that truth, he found peace, strength, and the undeniable knowledge that love, perseverance, and family would always be the foundation of his life and legacy.

Poem 1: Roots of Resilience

Under the storm, beneath the sky, deep in the rocks,

where silence lies, are those roots of strength unseen alone.

Holds firm when the wind and weather blow.

Rooted where the shadows pass,

In soil that's bruised and broken glass,

They reach from hurt into the light and bring inside what's good and right.

This is a seed that is sown in every storm. A whisper lost in the wind that moans.

This is a promise, then buried in the ground, waiting for the sun to turn up.

For resilience is a wicked embrace, a fierce, shimmering dance, Flame begets flesh and spirit from blood.

A testament to this life we love.

Hope it hums in the quiet rain, A lullaby in soul and pain,

Music of the future's aim, a steady drum that beats again.

No exile can dampen fire,

no distance can kill desire.

For hope and strength are entwined, a light never behind.

We wear scars as holy symbols of our light found through the dark.

In each descent, a rise anew,

Courage, steadfast in our view,

A tribute to all we have endured

A strength reborn, renewed, assured.

Roots of resilience, deep and wide,

Holding us steady through the tide

And from this soil where hope unites

We bloom anew; we claim our rights.

Poem 2: Heritage's Flame

In the still silence of midnight time,

Old stories flicker, not forgotten, nor old.

They dance like embers in the dark, A sacred fire, a vital spark.

The eternal flame of heritage burns deep,

A hushed tone lies in our hearts' inner keep,

The resonance of an echo from centuries old,

Reminding that roots in calamity are bold.

Ancestors speak softly and clearly,

Fill us with what we hold dear,

Through the dark of upturned doubt,

Their age-old wisdoms lay out.

Within each sound a holy hymn,

A tune that gives us strength within,

A strand that catches time and place,

Joining us in love's embrace.

No matter how far we wander away

Our roots will never ever decay,

They burn within us steady state,

As a fire that can't be stalemate.
A light upon the zephyrous brume,
A golden coupon ne'er to fume,
An alabaster brand of strife
Igniting hope in our lives.
Heritage a flame, eternal bright,
A legacy both pure and right,
A lode star for the eye to see,
The very core of you in me.

Poem 3: The Tapestry of Unity

A vibrant dance of colors there,

In the circumstances we share,

A tapestry of humankind, each thread a story intertwined.
From the four corners of the planet,

We draw our joy, pain, and value,

Numerous voices in concert,

Song practicing itself from a raindrop.
Echoes in the atmosphere,

Stories shared of smiles and tears,

Bitter roots and scars now healed,

Humanity's oneness revealed.
We join from places far apart,

Our past has left an aching mark.
In every hand, a dream to soar,

A glimmer of hope through shadowed doorways.

Building futures on light we share,

Together we will find our prayers.
The endless dance of roots and wings,

Intertwined in hope that sings,

Finding our path, hand in hand,

A new dawn is born every day.
A place where hope and love entwine,

You are a beauty, you are divine!

A work of art that only we can paint

Hope, joy, and a horizon both fade.
No longer strangers, but a thread,

A fabric strong, alive, and fed.

Bound by dreams, by courage, grace

A collective sacred space.
For in this tapestry we weave, lies the power to believe,

that every soul, in unity, creates a future rich and free.

Poem 4: Land and Spirit

Stories from times ever old,
echoes of the brave and bold,
My people's stories are retold.

Hands that know how to paint
Roots reaching deep beyond the heavens
Where spirits and angels are beckoning
To wings of gold who fly on knowing winds

I'd been seeking forgiveness
In Creation's cosmic out-breath
When my late wife called me again
To inhale some sacred humus.

Land and spirit, breath and core,
Remind me of who I was before,
Before the pain, before the fall.
This sacred truth that binds us all.

In every leaf and every tree
Lies the song of eternity
A rhapsody that never fades

A harmony that earth pervades.

A bond unbroken, true and deep,
A promise that my spirit keeps.
The essence of the earth's caress,
And lead me through in no less.

For in the land's eternal verse,
My old notebook is immersed,
A holy flame that will not die
Spirit and soil, my lullaby.

Poem 5: Love Beyond Borders

Love is a bridge over the infinite seas,
A holy road that stirs us with ease,
Connecting hearts in muted embrace,
A force divined no walls can efface.
It's a bridge made of hope and trust,
A gentle wind that whooshes dust,
Carrying dreams from soul to soul,
Making even broken pieces whole.
Love sings gently in the air,
So broad and deep from each to share.
A holy fire that reignites,
A constant beacon through the nights.
Its glow knows no borders,
Its flow knows no walls,
It travels like rivers in the night,
A force that makes light out of darkness.
In every soul, an ember burns
A flickering spark, the heart it turns
But with gentle winds of fate and chance

To grow into a wild romance

It's a chain that cannot be held,

A salve for every wound impelled,

A roaring yet sublime wave,

That cannot be enslaved.

Love knows no bounds; all is free

The key to our destiny, that boundless path

that leads us home, that shared dawn after night's gloom.

It is a sign without signs, the music that every heart finds.

Power that tears down each wall and raises us all,

both great and small. A love that knows no border, none of time,

A rhythm sacred, a rhyme divine,

The force of nature makes us connect

With me connect to you. In love's sweet arms,

We lose track. A park that leads us day by day,

a power that connects and makes us whole,

until the last star stops shining.

Author's Note

This story is my journey of discovery, a testament to the human spirit's ability to survive against all odds and to the power of love to change everything. It is a lesson that home is not only where we are from, but what we carry with us: stories, traditions, and principles that shape us. In a time when the world seems more divided than ever, I wish this story would open eyes and build bridges. People all over the world should follow their hearts rather than judge a book by its cover. It is fundamental to embrace our shared humanity and love each other for who we really are. These are the real Kings and Queens of life's Kingdom: Love, Respect, and Friendship. They can span oceans, close wounds, and leave a legacy that transcends time. May this story serve as a guide for those who long to belong and as a reminder that, no matter how far we journey into our lives, the people who love and support us will always tether us to soft, steady shores.

Letter to readers

As you finish this story, I encourage you to think about your own roots and the links that connect you to others. Consider the stories you bear, the traditions that make you who you are, and the love that bolsters you when times get tough. Never forget that true belonging is not only about being accepted in one place, but also about where you truly belong. And for me, that was always and will continue to be my mindset. Embrace the adventure and flow, honor your roots, and become a bridge of love and understanding in your life. Thank you for walking with me on this path. May you grow your strong roots and keep your heart open to the infinite possibilities of unity and hope.

www.ingramcontent.com/pod-product-compliance
Lightning Source LLC
LaVergne TN
LVHW010934110826
845149LV00013B/2599
* 9 7 8 1 9 7 2 0 0 4 2 3 4 *